She was having his baby....

Even in the darkness he could see that. He took her arm and looked her over. "Are you all right? Did they hurt you?"

She didn't answer. Instead she spat out, "There are men out there with guns who want to kill me and I have no idea why!"

"I'm not going to let anyone hurt you, Lily."

"Why is it that things never change with you? There's always danger."

"We don't have time for this now." Taking her hand, he tugged her deeper into the dark hall. "We have to get out of here."

She resisted. She'd had enough of the lifestyle Chase craved. Her baby came first now, and it needed stability. Something she'd never get from Chase, no matter how much she loved him. "I'm not going anywhere with you."

Hearing noises down the corridor, Chase pulled her against him, his breath hot and moist on her neck. His hand slid around to splay across her belly, reminding Lily of their child. "Like it or not," he breathed, "I'm your best hope of making it through the night."

LINDA CASTILLO

A BABY BEFORE DAWN

HARLEQUIN®

TORONTO • NEW YORK • LONDON
AMSTERDAM • PARIS • SYDNEY • HAMBURG
STOCKHOLM • ATHENS • TOKYO • MILAN • MADRID
PRAGUE • WARSAW • BUDAPEST • AUCKLAND

Special thanks and acknowledgment are given to
Linda Castillo for her contribution
to the LIGHTS OUT miniseries.

ISBN-13: 978-0-373-88774-3
ISBN-10:   0-373-88774-4

A BABY BEFORE DAWN

ABOUT THE AUTHOR

Linda Castillo knew at a very young age that she wanted to be a writer—and penned her first novel at the age of thirteen. She is the winner of numerous writing awards, including a Holt Medallion, a Golden Heart Award, a Daphne du Maurier and a nomination for the prestigious RITA® Award.

Linda loves writing edgy romantic suspense novels that push the envelope and that take her readers on a roller-coaster ride of breathtaking romance and thrilling suspense. She resides in Texas with her husband, four loveable dogs and an Appaloosa named George. For a complete list of her books, check out her Web site at www.lindacastillo.com. Contact her at books@lindacastillo.com. Or write her at P.O. Box 577, Bushland, Texas 79012.

Books by Linda Castillo

HARLEQUIN INTRIGUE

871—OPERATION: MIDNIGHT TANGO
890—OPERATION: MIDNIGHT ESCAPE
920—OPERATION: MIDNIGHT GUARDIAN
940—OPERATION: MIDNIGHT RENDEZVOUS
963—OPERATION: MIDNIGHT COWBOY
1000—A BABY BEFORE DAWN

Don't miss any of our special offers. Write to us at the following address for information on our newest releases.

Harlequin Reader Service
U.S.: 3010 Walden Ave., P.O. Box 1325, Buffalo, NY 14269
Canadian: P.O. Box 609, Fort Erie, Ont. L2A 5X3

CAST OF CHARACTERS

Chase Vickers—Seven and a half months ago, he walked away from the only woman he ever loved. But when her life is threatened by a madman, Chase is the only man who can help.

Lily Garrett—A down-to-earth emergency room nurse, all Lily ever wanted was family and security. All of that is threatened when someone tries to kill her.

Aidan Shea—The son of disgraced former mercenary Liam Shea, Aidan lives to avenge the people who framed his father.

Shane Peters—Chase's half brother deserted him when Chase was just a boy. Shane wants to make it up to him now, but Chase isn't so forgiving.

Ben Parker—An FBI agent, Ben does everything in his power to help Chase and Lily as they go on the run. But someone is leaking their whereabouts to the men who are trying to kill them. Is Ben friend or foe?

Ty Jones and Ethan Matalon—Part of the Eclipse brotherhood, these two men are Chase's best friends. Because of the blackout, Chase can reach neither Ty nor Ethan. Have the killers already gotten to them?

Chapter One

4:00 a.m., August 2
7 hours since the blackout began

It was going to be a long night.

Chase Vickers should have been accustomed to waiting. In his line of work he did enough of it. But he'd never developed much in the way of patience. He liked to move. More to the point, he liked speed. Lots of it. Tonight, however, parked in the looming shadow of Boston's Hancock Tower with the city in the midst of a blackout, he passed the minutes pacing as he waited for his passenger. Curbside, the sleek limo he drove part-time—and affectionately called Irma—purred like a big black cat.

Around him, plunged into darkness, the usually unflappable city of Boston was in a state of panic. Even at this hour the tower bustled with city police, Secret Service personnel and the occasional frightened civilian dressed to the nines. From the look of things, something big had gone down inside.

Chase had received the call for a client pickup just before 9:00 p.m. He was supposed to drive a foreign dignitary from Hancock Tower to Logan Airport. A simple enough assignment under most circumstances, anyway. Until the blackout hit en route. Traffic had crashed to a halt, and for the next three hours he'd maneuvered the big limo through spaces more suited to a Volkswagen. He'd dealt with an army of frightened motorists and angry cabbies, and dodged dozens of accidents caused by inoperative traffic lights.

Chase was comfortable in the dark and chaos. When he wasn't driving dignitaries and high-ranking government officials to various destinations—most requiring a driver with a high-security clearance—he spent his days on mercenary missions for Eclipse, a secret organization he and three other of his Special Forces buddies had formed years ago. For a price, the band of brothers took on assignments the CIA, FBI and other elite military forces couldn't get done. The kinds of covert operations that never made the newspapers.

Lately, those missions were the only time Chase felt truly alive.

He stood at the rear of the limo, taking in the chaos, wondering about its source. This was more than just a blackout situation. The arrival of additional Secret Service told him something significant had transpired. Was it related to the black-tie affair atop the tower? He'd read about the event. Something to do with a trade agreement…

Pulling out his cell phone, he was about to make some calls to see if he could get some answers when a chirp alerted him to an incoming text message. He hit Receive and watched the words scroll across the display.

Are you afraid of the dark?

The jagged scar above his left eye throbbed as the meaning of the words registered. Four years in the Special Forces and numerous missions for Eclipse had taught him to take every threat seriously, regardless of its source or how vague. The truth of the matter was, he'd made some enemies over the years. He'd ticked off some very dangerous people who would probably like nothing more than to pay him back in spades.

Chase knew whom to call. As much as Chase didn't want to turn to his older brother—half brother, he corrected with a sneer—Shane Peters did seem to have his finger on the pulse. He punched in Shane's number from memory. Five rings and his call went to voice mail. Another oddity— his half brother almost always answered his phone. What the hell was going on?

"Hey, it's Vic," he said, using the nickname known exclusively by his Special Forces and Eclipse counterparts. "Call me."

He was about to get back in the limo when a thin young man with dark hair exited the tower and approached. The tuxedo told Chase the man was part of the black-tie affair. More than likely the dignitary he'd been hired to drive to Logan Airport.

He studied the man's face; a flash of familiarity gave him pause. Something about the eyes. But as the man drew closer Chase decided he was mistaken. He had a near photographic memory; he would have recalled meeting this man. His green eyes and black hair made his face a memorable one. But Chase knew both could be easily altered.

He put on a smile and started toward his passenger. "Hell of a night for a blackout."

"It's a madhouse in there." The man glanced at the limo with the admiration of a man who appreciated fine machinery. "You must be Chase Vickers."

"The one and only." Because he would require his passenger to do the same, Chase pulled out his wallet and flashed his ID and security badge.

The man fumbled with his own wallet. "I'm Sam Michaels."

The name confirmed this man was, indeed, his assigned passenger, but Chase looked carefully at the driver's license and accompanying photo ID anyway, putting both to memory. Samuel Michaels. Washington, D.C. Personal aide to the ambassador of South Africa. DOB 06-06-1981.

Confident everything was in order, Chase walked to the passenger door and opened it, ushering his client inside. "Logan Airport?"

The man smiled wryly as he climbed into the limo's plush backseat. "Not that any of the airlines are operational in this blackout."

"Where you headed?"

"London. Sometime tomorrow, if I'm lucky."

"Hopefully, the power outage won't last much longer."

"Any idea what happened?"

Chase shook his head. "Most of the radio stations were knocked off the air, but some are bound to have backup generators that are up and running by now. I'll see if I can pick up a newscast."

Closing the door, he crossed in front of the vehicle and slid behind the wheel. Getting to the airport was going to be a challenge.

Chase wasn't overly concerned. A speed freak and racing enthusiast, he'd never met a road or highway he couldn't traverse no matter what the conditions.

He pulled onto the street, squeezing Irma between a city bus and a taxicab with inches to spare. The move elicited the simultaneous blare of a dozen horns but, like most professional drivers, he didn't pay them any heed.

A second glance in the mirror told him Samuel Michaels was not a nervous passenger. Probably a good thing since getting him to Logan was going to take nothing less than a miracle.

"There's a bar in the forward cabinet," Chase said. "Help yourself."

Sam Michaels smiled. "Looks like I might need a nip or two by the time we get there."

"Hang on. Bump ahead." Chase took the limo onto the curb to get around a BMW that had played chicken with a Ford pickup and lost.

He was so focused on maneuvering through the jumble of cars that for several minutes Chase did nothing but drive. Traffic eased marginally when he turned onto Interstate 93. Deciding to avoid the Ted Williams Tunnel for fear of an immovable traffic jam, he headed north toward the financial district.

When he finally took a second to look in his rearview mirror to check on his passenger, he found himself staring into the barrel of a sleek Ruger Mark III .22 pistol replete with a magazine release and front and rear sights. A killer's gun.

"What the hell are you doing?" Chase said with outer calm as his gaze met his passenger's.

"Repaying a debt."

"What debt?" Adrenaline punched him like a fist, but he kept his eyes and voice level. "Who the hell are you?"

"It doesn't matter who I am, *Vic.* I know who you are. That's the important thing."

Vic.

The only people who called him that were his teammates from Special Forces, three of whom comprised Eclipse. Once again his mind scrolled through possible enemies he'd made over the years, but he couldn't recall any escapees or recently released inmates.

"What do you want?" Chase asked.

The man leaned forward. "You're about to find out what it feels like to lose everything that matters to you."

"What are you talking about?"

The man's smile chilled him.

Chase knew it was crazy, but Lily came to mind. He hadn't seen her for almost eight months, but the time apart hadn't dulled his feelings for her. Lily Garrett was the only thing in this world that truly mattered to him. Had this man somehow found out that he'd once been involved with her? Was he going to hurt Lily to get back at Chase for some perceived wrong?

Knowing this wasn't going to end nicely, Chase swung the steering wheel hard to the right. He caught a glimpse of his passenger trying to hold on while sliding sideways on the backseat. The gun came up. "Stop or I'll blow your head off!"

Steel screamed against steel when the limo careened into a parked delivery van. The man's temple snapped hard against the side window. Strapped in securely with his safety belt, Chase jammed the limo into Reverse and hit the gas. He saw a flash of blue steel in the mirror and jerked the wheel hard to the left. The passenger slid to the opposite side. Chase slammed on the brake and the man's head struck the partially open Plexiglas divider separating the passenger compartment from the cab.

Ramming the limo into Park, Chase unbuckled his seat belt, spun and jammed his torso through the small opening. He reached for Michaels and snagged the collar of his tux. Cursing, the man scrambled back, grappling for his weapon. He tried to get off a shot, but Chase shoved his arm and the bullet went wide, blowing a hole the size of his thumb through the roof.

"Now that wasn't very nice," Chase growled through clenched teeth.

"Maybe I want you to be alive when we kill her," the man snarled.

Her.

The man had to be referring to Lily. Panic gripped Chase. Was this thug planning to use her to get to him? The thought of some goon hurting her in the name of revenge made him break a cold sweat.

Too late, he saw the gun come up. He reached for the muzzle to deflect it, but because of his awkward position, he wasn't fast enough. A second gunshot rent the night. The bullet struck his arm like a five-hundred-degree baseball bat slamming a home run. But he didn't have time to feel the high-voltage shock of pain. The son of a bitch was already lining up for another shot.

Pulling away, Chase shoved the gearshift into Drive and floored the accelerator. The limo jumped forward like a big predator. The engine roared, the RPMs redlining. Chase cut the wheel. The front quarter panel clipped a streetlight. The limo spun. Chase saw the man slide across the backseat and crash into the door. Jamming the limo into Reverse, he hit the gas. The vehicle shot backward like a racehorse out of the gate and slammed into a parked car hard enough to whip his skull against the headrest.

Knowing this was probably his last chance to gain control of the situation, he reached for his own weapon beneath his seat and swung open the door. By the time he was out and had yanked open the passenger door, Michaels had slipped out the opposite side.

"Halt!" Assuming a shooter's stance, Chase took aim over the limo's roof and fired off three shots. But the man moved too fast, darting around cars and through the crowd. Within seconds, darkness swallowed him.

Chase stood trembling, wondering what the hell had just happened. The pain in his arm snapped him back to the situation at hand. He glanced down, saw blood soaking his sleeve.

"Damn," he muttered. "Ruined my best shirt."

But his mind churned with the threats the man had made.

I want you to be alive when we kill her.

The words echoed in his head like some terrible mantra. He hadn't mentioned a name, but Chase knew the bastard was talking about Lily.

Jerking open the door, he slid behind the wheel. The engine had died. He turned the key and pumped the gas, but the motor only wheezed like a sick cow. Frustrated and more scared than he'd been in a very long time, he rapped his palm hard against the wheel.

"You picked a hell of a time to let me down, Irma."

Chase threw open the door. Ignoring the blare of horns and throngs of stranded motorists, he broke into a dead run toward the only woman he'd ever loved.

IT WAS GOING TO BE a long night.

Lily Garrett rushed down the wide corridor toward Examination Room Two, her footfalls hushed on the tile floor. The hall was dimly lit, the only light coming from overhead emergency bulbs powered by generators that had kicked on automatically when the blackout hit.

She glanced at the wall clock to see it was just after four in the morning, and wondered vaguely when the power would be restored. An emergency room nurse at New England Medical Center, she'd been hard at it for sixteen hours. Her feet felt every hour she'd been on them. Being seven-and-a-half months pregnant wasn't helping matters. Her stamina wasn't what it used to be. Her body simply didn't move as quickly as it once had. To make matters worse, the baby had chosen tonight of all nights to kick a field goal every minute or so.

As always, the thought of the child growing inside her made her think of Chase. For months she'd done her utmost to get him out of her mind, working many a night to the brink of collapse. When she wasn't working, she spent much of her time with friends. Anything to fill up that great big hole in her life where he'd once been. But despite her efforts, he always found his way back. He was the kind of man a woman never forgot. The kind of man a woman went to her grave loving, no matter how many times he hurt her.

Damn Chase Vickers and his addiction to adrenaline.

Her decision to walk away hadn't been an easy one. It wasn't until she'd found out she was pregnant that she'd stuck to her guns and totally cut him out of her life. What kind of father would he make? The kind that turned a woman into a widow and left a child emotionally traumatized.

At any given time he was running off to war zones all over the globe. Any woman who loved him would always be left at home, wondering when he was going to come back. Wondering *if* he would come back. And she would inevitably pray that when he did, it wasn't in a body bag.

Not Lily. She and her baby were better off alone. It wouldn't be easy. But even as a single parent, she would be able to give her child stability. Chase Vickers didn't know the meaning of the word.

Shoving thoughts of him aside the way she had every day for too many months to count, she yanked open the privacy curtain of the exam room and stepped inside. Four people had arrived a few minutes ago, victims of an elevator that had plummeted two stories when the power failed. The three women suffered various broken bones and bruises. But the man had sustained a closed head wound and was in serious condition.

Lily rushed to the gurney where the frazzled-looking emergency room doctor and respiratory therapist worked frantically to stabilize their patient. Operating on instinct, she noted vitals, called radiology for the second time and watched the emergency team work.

A firm hand on her shoulder turned her around. "Lily, if you don't take a break, it's going to be *you* flat on your back."

She looked into her friend's eyes and smiled. Karen Turner was a veteran nurse and damn good at what she did. With four children of her own and her first grandchild on the way, Karen knew the ropes when it came to pregnancy, too. She never hesitated to speak her mind, and Lily loved her for it.

"I mean it, kiddo. You've been here since noon," Karen said. "That's sixteen hours, honey. Go to the break room. Lie down on the cot for a while."

Acknowledging the ache in her lower back, Lily nodded. "If I wasn't so tired, I might argue with you."

Karen laughed. "We got things under control here. Now scoot."

"Only if you let me bring you a cup of coffee."

"Sweet and black, honey." She grinned. "Just like me."

Smiling, Lily left the emergency room. The closer she got to the nurse's lounge, the more she realized she'd overdone it. Again. Her ankles hurt. Her swollen belly felt tight. Her back ached. But with casualties pouring in because of blackout-related accidents, she couldn't leave.

Deciding to make a stop at the cafeteria first, she veered right and headed toward the bank of elevators. The kitchen was closed at this hour, but she could at least get something from one of the vending machines.

The elevator doors chimed open and two orderlies hustled out. Lily stepped inside and hit the button, taking that precious time to massage her aching back on the ride down to the basement. Thoughts of a turkey sandwich on rye, and maybe a chocolate cupcake for dessert, enticed her as the doors slid open.

To her surprise the foyer was deserted. Beyond the double doors, the cafeteria stood in near darkness, the only light coming from auxiliary bulbs and four Exit signs, which switched on automatically when the power failed.

The darkness was odd even at this hour. New England Medical Center was a large, bustling hospital and teaching facility, like a self-contained city that never slept. The cafeteria was usually busy, but perhaps the generator had been diverted to handle the rush of incoming emergency patients or operating facilities.

"I just hope the vending machines work," she muttered as she dug a couple of bills from her pocket and started for the nearest source of food.

She'd just fed a dollar into the machine when a sound behind her spun her around.

Lily wasn't nervous about the dark, and she was hardly ever frightened. But standing alone in the shadowy cafeteria, gooseflesh raced down her arms.

"Is someone there?" she called out.

When no one answered, she shook her head and turned back to the vending machine. "You ate my dollar," she muttered.

The shuffle of shoes against tile made her turn again. In the dim light coming from the kitchen behind the serving counter, she saw the unmistakable silhouette of a man dash past the doorway.

The gooseflesh she'd felt earlier transformed into a chill. Before her pregnancy, she might have confronted him, demanding to know what he was doing there. Now, however, Lily was much more safety conscious. Before reacting, she always took into consideration the well-being of her unborn child.

The hospital was generally a secure work environment. But she knew many times blackouts brought out looters—and worse. Better to get back upstairs as quickly as possible and notify security.

Never taking her eyes from the kitchen area, Lily backed toward the nearest exit. She was midway there when she heard a sound behind her. Uneasiness mushroomed into fear when she spun and saw the man's silhouette just twenty feet away.

"Lily Garrett." He uttered her name in a terrible whisper.

All she could think was that he knew her name. "Who are you?"

The sound of a pistol being cocked hit her like a cattle prod. Lily knew nothing about guns, but she'd seen enough shoot-'em-up movies to discern the sound of a bullet being chambered.

Instinct propelled her to the adjacent door. She swept past benches and tables at a dead run. Her shoes pounded the tile as she burst through the door and down the corridor at a dangerous speed. At the elevator, she slammed her fist against the Up button. But there was no time to wait for the car. Glancing over her shoulder, she saw the man's shadow at the cafeteria door.

The gunshot blast rendered her momentarily paralyzed with fear. Plaster flew from the wall less than a foot from where she stood. *Dear God, he's shooting at me!* An Exit light over the stairwell door at the end of the hall beckoned. Lily sprinted toward it. Panicked gasps broke from her lips as she ran. Behind her, she heard footfalls and knew he was coming after her.

She swung open the door and hit the steps running, taking two at a time. At the landing she paused to catch her breath. Suddenly, the door below burst open and banged wide. In the glare of the Exit light she saw the silhouette of the man, his face darting toward her, the dark shadow of a gun rising.

Lily spun and clambered up the stairs, terror and utter disbelief ripping through her with each step. All she could think of was her baby. But in order to save her child, she had to first save herself.

The hospital lobby was on the first floor. Even this time of night it would be filled with people. Lily shoved open the door. Dim emergency lighting illuminated the huge atrium.

"Help!" she screamed as she ran toward the information desk. "Gun!"

Startled glances swung her way. Two clerks looked up as she dashed to the counter. Lily set both hands on the Formica top, breathless with adrenaline and fear. "There's a man with a gun!" she shouted.

One of the clerks grabbed the phone. "I'll notify security."

Lily looked toward the stairwell door and the bank of elevators, but the gunman was nowhere in sight. Had he followed her? Was he already amongst the throngs of people in the lobby?

"Where is he?" the second clerk asked.

Lily scanned the atrium. Several groups of people gathered near the potted palms in the center of the room. A few more stood near the gift shop. Beyond the glass revolving door, the lights of an ambulance flashed red and blue.

"I don't know," Lily said. "He was in the cafeteria. He had a gun and fired a shot at me. I think he may have followed me up here."

"Honey, maybe you ought to sit down."

The older clerk rose and moved around the counter. "I called nine-one-one."

Lily didn't think the cops could get there fast enough if the gunman decided to start shooting. She took one more look around the room, but didn't see the man. "Where's security?"

"They're on the way," said the older clerk. "They've been tied up all night with this blackout. People get crazy when it's dark. Whole city's gone mad."

A gunshot shattered the relative peace of the lobby. On instinct, Lily crouched low, shocked the man would open fire with so many people around. In her peripheral vision she saw both clerks duck. To her right, a young security officer ran toward her, his pistol ready in his hand.

"Halt! Security! Drop the weapon now!"

Thwack! Thwack! Thwack!

The security officer clutched his shoulder and went down. Lily saw blood on his uniform. She looked around wildly but couldn't spot the shooter. Screams filled the atrium as people scrambled for cover.

Dropping to her hands and knees, she crawled toward a grouping of furniture and potted plants. She could feel her breaths coming hard and fast. Her heart pounded so hard she thought it might hammer its way right out of her chest.

Setting her hand protectively over her abdomen, she peered over the back of the sofa. The lobby had gone nearly silent, as if holding its breath in anticipation of the next burst of violence. The shooter was nowhere in sight. Had he gone? After her encounter with him in the cafeteria, she was surprised he'd ventured into a crowded area. Unless she was the target.

The notion was ludicrous considering her humdrum lifestyle. These days all she did was work, in anticipation of the birth of her child. She was saving as much money as possible so she could give her baby the security she deserved.

Lily might have believed all of this was random. That she'd just been in the wrong place at the wrong time. Then she remembered he'd whispered her name, and she knew this was not indiscriminate. But why on earth would someone target her?

She thought about the security officer who'd been shot. From where she crouched she could see him on the floor. Clutching his shoulder, he spoke into his radio. The need to help him taunted her. If she hadn't been pregnant, she might have attempted it or at least tried to find an EMT to help her move him out of the line of fire. But she had to think of her child now. That meant staying put until help arrived. Where the hell were the police?

Movement to her right snagged her attention. Adrenaline burst through her when she realized it was the gunman. He walked calmly, brazenly among the frightened, cowering people, pointing his weapon but not shooting. As if he were searching for someone in particular.

Looking for *her?*

Terror closed over her like a giant, smothering hand. Closing her eyes, Lily fought a rise of panic. From his bulk, she could tell this wasn't the same man she'd encountered in the basement, which meant there was more than one shooter. What in the name of God was going on here?

Gun drawn, the man systematically searched the atrium. People whimpered as he passed them by. Lily prayed he didn't shoot. A terrible sense of helplessness descended over her. Crouching lower, she raised her head and peered over the sofa back. The shooter was less than thirty feet away, his eyes narrowed and scanning, the gun ready at his side.

Knowing she had mere seconds before he discovered her hiding place, she looked around for another. The front revolving doors were too far away; she'd have to cover too much open ground to reach them. Behind her, a dark hallway led to the public restrooms and a bank of pay phones. She didn't get down here often, but she was pretty sure there was an emergency exit at the end. If she could reach the hall, she could sneak out the door undetected. But she had to move. Now.

Never taking her eyes from the man with the gun, she crawled backward toward the darkened corridor. Twenty feet away, he ordered several people facedown on the floor. Lily prayed he spared them, but she didn't stop moving.

She was midway to her destination when a subtle noise from behind her nearly stopped her heart. She looked over her shoulder to see the dark figure of another man rush her. All she could think was that there was a third shooter, and her pulse went wild. A yelp escaped her an instant before he pressed his hand to her mouth.

"If you want to live, don't make a sound," he said, and dragged her into the corridor.

Chapter Two

If not for his military training, Chase would have surely walked into a bullet. It wasn't the first time his instincts had saved his life. Maybe this time, they'd saved Lily's life, too.

He almost didn't see her. Not because of the darkness or the throngs of frightened people. When he'd entered the hospital ten minutes ago, he hadn't been looking for a pregnant woman.

But a man never forgot certain things about a woman he'd once loved. Chase had spotted Lily from thirty feet away in near total darkness. Despite her bulging midsection, he'd known immediately it was her. He would know her if he were blind and deaf. He would know her by touch alone. By smell. By the way she breathed.

He couldn't believe she was pregnant. Couldn't believe she'd moved on to another man so quickly. He had to bank a quick rise of jealousy.

But there was no time for petty emotions now. From the balcony above the atrium lobby, he'd counted two shooters, possibly three. He didn't like the odds, but he'd faced worse. For now, he had to focus on moving her out of there without either of them getting shot.

Lily struggled against him as he pulled her into the darkened hall. Terror and panic came off her in waves. She thought he was one of the gunmen, that he meant her harm, but there'd been no time to identify himself let alone talk her into letting him help her.

"It's Chase," he whispered. "Calm down. You know I won't hurt you."

She went still, but he could feel her trembling violently. Her breaths came in fast, short bursts from her nose. He'd approached her from behind and wrapped his right arm around her abdomen, placing his left hand over her mouth. Her body pressed flush against his. It was more lush than he remembered and so soft and warm that for a moment all he could think of was sinking into her and never letting her go. That the old attraction was still sharp after so many months shocked him almost as much as her pregnancy.

"I'm going to take my hand from your mouth," he said in a low voice. "Don't scream or those goons with guns are going to come calling. You got that?"

She nodded.

Slowly, he removed his hand.

She turned to face him. In the semidarkness her big green eyes looked black against her pale complexion. As always, she'd pulled her long curly red hair into a no-nonsense ponytail at her nape. She looked the same as last time he'd seen her. The same as in every dream he'd had about her in the months they'd been apart. Except for the soft roundness of her belly.

"What are you doing here?" she whispered.

Because he wasn't quite sure how to answer, he eased her to arm's length and looked her over. "Are you all right? Did they hurt you?"

"I'm okay." Her eyes flicked to the lobby. "There are two men out there with guns who want to kill me and I have no idea why."

"I'm not going to let anyone hurt you," he said.

She noticed the blood on his sleeve, and her eyes softened. But realization dawned and the softness quickly transformed into anger. "My God, you're part of this."

"That's not how it is."

She looked as if she wanted to hit him. "Things never change with you, do they, Chase?"

"This is no mission," he said, hating that his tone was defensive. His work with Eclipse and his penchant for risk taking had been points of contention between them from the beginning of their relationship.

"Save it," she said.

"We don't have time for this now, Lily." Taking her hand, he tugged her more deeply into the hall. She resisted, but her efforts were token and he easily muscled her to the alcove outside the restrooms. "We have to get out of here right now."

"I'm not going anywhere with you."

"You don't have a choice, damn it." He glanced toward the lobby. "Those bastards mean business."

"Who are they? Why are they doing this? Why do they want to hurt me?" Her questions came in a flurry.

"I don't know," he said. "We'll figure it out later. For now, I need to get you out of here."

"Chase, damn it—"

He cut her off, ushering her to the farthest wall of the alcove. "For once in your life listen to me." He glanced toward the lobby. "Stay put. I need to see where they are."

Pressing his back flat against the wall, he sidled to the hall entrance and peered into the lobby. The two gunmen stood in the center of the atrium, looking around. Chase slipped back to the alcove.

Lily had ventured only a few feet, her hand placed protectively over her abdomen. She'd always been strong willed and capable, not the kind of woman who needed or wanted protecting. But standing there with fear in her eyes and a baby growing inside her, she looked incredibly vulnerable. The need to protect her rose inside him in a dangerous tide.

"Let's go."

She didn't resist as he pulled her toward the emergency exit at the end of the hall. A sign above the push bar on the door told him an alarm would sound if the door was opened. Since it was the only exit they could reach without being seen, he didn't have a choice but to take it and hope the alarm had been rendered inoperative because of the blackout.

"If that alarm is intact, all hell is going to break loose when we go through this door," he said.

"In case you haven't noticed, hell already *has* broken loose," she shot back.

"Can you run?"

She glanced down at her belly. "What do you think?"

"I think you don't have a choice."

Chase hit the security bar and shoved

open the door. A shrill alarm split the air. "Run!" he whispered.

The door opened to the sidewalk on Harrison Avenue. Abandoned cars that had run out of gas during the massive traffic jam that had followed the blackout littered the street. Flames flickered from a drum where someone burned garbage, but there was no one in sight. The street was pitch-black and eerily quiet.

"This way."

Chase pulled her into a run, and they headed north on Harrison at a fast clip. She didn't complain, but he could feel her struggling to keep up. She'd once been quite athletic, so he knew it was her pregnancy slowing her down.

"Come on," he said. "You can do it."

"I'm moving as fast as I can," she said between pants.

Behind them, a shout echoed, telling him at least one of the gunmen had spotted them. "Faster!" Chase shouted. "Run!"

A volley of gunfire shattered the night. A yelp escaped Lily when a bullet ricocheted off the brick facade of a building inches from her head. Terror whipped through Chase. He glanced at her, saw blood on her cheek and his heart stopped dead in his chest.

Lily must have noticed his expression. "Piece of brick knicked me," she said. "Keep moving, Vickers."

"That a girl," he said, and urged her faster.

Midway down the block, the yawning black mouth of an alley beckoned. Praying they didn't encounter a dead end, Chase cut right and they traversed it at a reckless speed, their footfalls echoing off the brick walls on either side. Considering the advanced stage of her pregnancy, Lily was amazingly fast on her feet. But not fast enough. Twenty yards in, another gunshot rang out.

"They're still shooting at us!" she cried.

"Keep running!"

"I'm spent, Chase. I can't go much farther."

Cursing, he pulled his pistol from the waistband of his slacks and returned fire blindly, hoping it would be enough to slow their pursuers. All the while the thought of her falling to a bullet tortured him with horrific images.

The alley opened to another side street. Chase headed right toward Chinatown, a bustling section of the city where foot traffic, greengrocers, fish markets and ethnic shops crowded the narrow streets. Left without a vehicle, he figured their best hope of eluding their pursuers was to get lost in the crowd.

"Chase, tell me what's going on." The words puffed out on each breath as they cut down Kneeland Street.

"I don't know," he said.

Digging in her heels, she stopped and jerked her hand from his. "Don't lie to me, damn it. We're not talking about just me. We're talking about this baby."

He didn't need to be reminded of that. The fact hadn't left his mind since the moment he'd spotted her. Setting his hands on her shoulders, he looked into her eyes and recapped everything that had happened back at Hancock Tower. "I checked the passenger's ID and everything was cool." Remembering, he gritted his teeth, incensed with himself for having let the man get the jump on him. "Until he pulled a gun."

"And you have no idea why?"

"No."

"Why did you come to the hospital?" she demanded. "Why involve me?"

Looking left and right, he guided her to an alley that would take them into the heart of Chinatown. "When the guy was in the limo, he said some things that made me think he was going to hurt you."

"Hurt me?" She laughed, but it was a tense, humorless sound. "Why? What made you jump to that conclusion?"

"He told me I was about to lose everything that I—" Realizing what he'd almost said, Chase cut the words short. "He mentioned you by name."

Even in the semidarkness he saw the color drain from her face. "I don't understand. Why me? I don't even know these people."

"Evidently, they know me."

"But we haven't been together for…"

Something pinged in his brain. "Seven-and-a-half months," he finished.

But Chase's mind was already jumping ahead to something he'd been wondering about since the moment he'd spotted her in the hospital atrium. Until now he hadn't had a chance to work out the timing of her pregnancy. Looking at her, on some primal level, he suddenly knew.

He *knew*.

His heart raced. Not because of the men with guns, but because he was remembering the last time he'd been with Lily. Seven-and-a-half months ago…

When he looked at her, he saw the answer in her eyes. He saw the truth and it shattered him as surely as any bullet. "Is the baby mine?" he asked hollowly.

His own words stunned him. He stared at her, feeling his world shift on its axis.

Lily stared back, her green eyes startled and slightly defiant. A lock of curly red hair had come loose from her ponytail. She'd always hated her hair, but he still dreamed of it. His fingers itched to tuck the errant strand behind her ear, but he didn't dare touch her. Once he did, he wasn't sure he'd be able to stop.

"No," she said quickly. "I—I had an affair shortly after we parted ways. I was…careless."

The denial rang false in every way. Chase knew better than anyone that Lily wasn't the kind of woman to jump from one man's bed to another. That could only mean one thing: The baby was his.

His.

Holy Moses. The supposition slammed into him like a Mack truck traveling at a high rate of speed. The scar above his eye, courtesy of shrapnel in Afghanistan, throbbed again.

"You're lying," he heard himself say.

That she didn't deny it drove home the cold hard truth of it. He felt as if he'd just been punched between the eyes with a set of brass knuckles. "I deserved to know the truth."

"Yes," she agreed. "You did."

"Then why—"

She gestured angrily toward the dangers behind them. "Look at what you've brought into my life. Men with guns. That's *exactly* why I didn't tell you. This baby, *my* baby, deserves to be safe. I put her well-being above the truth. Above you. For that, I'm sorry. But your knowing changes nothing."

"The hell it doesn't."

"You have no say in the matter."

Chase wanted to talk about this. A thousand emotions churned inside him in a kaleidoscope of shock and regret and newfound optimism. But there was no time to voice any of them. They had to get out of this alley and to a safe place. "We can't discuss this here."

He reached for her hand, but she pulled away. "I'm not going anywhere with you," she repeated.

For the first time, Chase's temper kicked in. He was tired of being blamed for all that was bad and wrong in the world. Even more tired of being kept in the dark and denied the things that mattered most. So what if he had a dangerous job? Someone had to keep the bad guys away. "If you care so much about that baby, you'll be reasonable."

"Don't you dare try to manipulate me

using this baby," she hissed. "There's nothing reasonable about any of what's happened."

"Maybe not. But you know I won't let anything happen to you."

"How can you say that? It's because of you that we're in danger to begin with."

The words stung, but he didn't let himself react. There was no time for emotion or blame or the rehashing of ancient history. "I'm the only reason you're alive right now. Like it or not, I'm your best hope of making it through the night."

LILY COULD BARELY HEAR him over the hard thrum of her heart. She hadn't wanted Chase to know about the baby, but she'd never been a good liar, especially when it came to him. There was no denying the timing of it. She and Chase had been together seven-and-a-half months ago. She knew lying was wrong. But for the first time in her life, she hadn't cared. Since the instant she'd found out she was pregnant, the baby had come first. She'd done what

she had to do and accepted the consequences of her actions.

She just hadn't expected it to be so damn
hard.

"These people want you, Chase, not
me," she said. "Wouldn't it be safer if you
walked away from us and left us alone?"

His jaw tightened. "They know they can
get to me through you. If I cut you loose
now, they'll be on you like wolves on a
lamb." Stepping close, he set his hand
against her cheek. "There's no way in hell
I'm going to let that happen."

"Chase—"

"If I walk away, I may as well put the gun
to your head and pull the trigger myself," he
cut in. "You're a target now. I'm sorry it went
down like this. I wish I could change things,
but I can't. Until I figure out who these
bastards are, you need me to stay alive."

Anger burst through the gnarly layers of
fear. "That's exactly why I didn't—" She
cut the words off abruptly, shocked that
she'd nearly said them aloud.

But he finished for her. "Tell me about
the baby?"

Lily couldn't answer. Staring into his striking topaz eyes, she felt the old feelings begin to churn. A cauldron of anger and attraction and something deeper she would not acknowledge. But those feelings were tempered with the certainty that wherever Chase went, danger followed. With a child to think of, Lily could not let herself be drawn into the maelstrom of his life.

Shouting from a newspaper kiosk across the street saved her from having to answer. Chase glanced over his shoulder, his head cocked, his body going stone still.

"My God," he said.

"What is it?"

"Vice President Davis has been kidnapped."

"Is that what this blackout is all about?" she asked, shocked by the news. "Someone was after the vice president?"

"He was at the black-tie ball where I picked up the guy who ambushed me."

"Do you think those gunmen back there are somehow involved in the kidnapping?"

"I'm going to find out." He reached for

his cell phone, hit a button with his thumb and cursed.

"What is it?" Lily asked.

"Battery's dead."

She might have laughed if the situation hadn't been so dire. "What about Irma? Can you recharge the battery using the cigarette lighter?"

His eyes softened at her mention of the limo. "Too far away. I wrecked her not far from the Hancock Tower."

She looked around the narrow, crowded streets of Chinatown, feeling uncomfortably exposed. "What do we do now?"

He glanced over his shoulder. "We need to get off the street and stay out of sight until I can figure out what's going on."

"You think they followed us?"

"Even if they didn't, it's only a matter of time until they start looking in this area."

A chill swept over her at the thought of some unseen gunman hunting them down like animals. Already she loved her child more than her own life. As much as she didn't want to admit it, Chase was right. She needed him to stay alive.

Lily started when he took her hand. Her initial reaction was to pull away: she couldn't risk getting too close to him. Chase Vickers was her one and only weakness, the one man in the world who could make her lose her head and forget about doing the right thing. With the baby to worry about, she couldn't risk letting down her guard.

But she allowed him to lead her through a narrow courtyard, past a smattering of quaint shops, most of which were closed. A few of the die-hard shopkeepers who'd kept their stores open stood outside on the sidewalk, chatting in Chinese.

Lily and Chase reached a main thoroughfare. Cars jammed the intersection, engines rumbling, horns blaring. The smell of exhaust filled the still night air. Abruptly, Chase stopped. The next thing Lily knew he had grasped both her arms and ushered her quickly toward a narrow courtyard.

"What is it?" she whispered.

He pushed her against the brick of an old building and placed himself between her and the street. "We've got company."

A deep chill passed through her body. She could almost *feel* the pistol sights leveled on her heart. Unnerved, Lily leaned against the brick and tried to catch her breath.

"Where?" she asked, resisting the urge to duck.

"Southwest corner. By the newsstand."

She followed his gaze. Sure enough, the gunmen she'd encountered in the cafeteria stood at the corner, talking into a cell phone and gesturing angrily. She wished she could hear what he was saying because she was almost certain it had to do with Chase and her.

"What do we do now?" she whispered.

"I need to get my hands on a phone."

Spinning, he urged her into a run. They sprinted through the courtyard, past a rusty fire escape and the darkened windows of a seafood shop where selections and prices were written in Chinese.

They ran for what seemed like forever. But Lily didn't think about the discomfort or fatigue. All she could think about were the armed gunmen who obviously meant her harm. She'd always known something like this would happen. How could Chase do this to her and the baby? How could he place them in danger like this?

At the end of the block, she pulled her hand from his. Bending, she gulped deep breaths until the aching in her back subsided.

"Are you all right?" he asked.

She wasn't all right. Not by a long shot. She was frightened and angry and worried. Her physical stamina had long since run its course. "I can't keep up this pace," she said between pants.

"Are you in pain?"

"No, I'm just…exhausted."

Setting his hand protectively on the small of her back, he looked around, his topaz eyes scanning the surrounding shops and fire escapes that laced the old buildings like steel spiderwebs. When his gaze met hers, Lily saw concern and a tenderness she didn't want to acknowledge.

"There's a homeless shelter a few blocks away," he said. "We can rest there and try to come up with a game plan."

"All right."

Avoiding the more populated areas, they stuck to the shadows beneath colorful awnings and darkened neon signs. Lily usually loved Chinatown. She walked it often, buying fresh vegetables and fish when she had time to cook. But tonight, the narrow streets and alleys seemed ominous. Every stranger they passed seemed dangerous. At every corner, she found herself looking for men with guns.

Even coolheaded Chase appeared uneasy. He held her hand a little too tightly. At every intersection he made her stop so he could check both ways, even scanning the tops of the buildings and fire escapes before they crossed the street. All the while his eyes took in every detail, assessed every person they passed.

This wasn't like Chase. He was usually the kind of man who jumped first and thought about consequences later. Tonight, his recklessness had been replaced with a caution she'd never before seen. She didn't want to think about what that meant. Was he concerned for her and her child's safety? Had he changed? Lily didn't think so.

She knew he cared for her. That he would protect her with his life. But it was too little, too late. Their relationship had already been shattered beyond repair.

At the north end of Chinatown, they passed an Asian man walking a fat brown Labrador retriever. Chase surprised her by stopping him and speaking in fluent Chinese. But then she'd learned to expect the unexpected from him. He was so unpredictable, so complex and intense, Lily had always felt a little out of her element when she was with him.

Chase removed his wallet and dug out two twenty-dollar bills. The man shook his head. Chase dug out two more twenties. Smiling, the man handed him his cell phone and gave a slight bow of his head.

"Expensive phone," she muttered.

"Worth its weight in gold if I can find out what's going on and get us some help." He motioned toward a dilapidated building at the end of the block. A hand-painted sign welcomed them to the Joy Family Shelter of Boston.

The homeless shelter was nestled in a

brick structure that had once been a textile factory. Plywood splattered with graffiti covered the windows. A colorful mural depicting a Chinese parade replete with fire-breathing dragons graced the brick facade.

At the door a white-haired man with a tiny matching goatee smiled at them. "Welcome to Joy Family Shelter," he said in broken English.

Chase dug another twenty from his wallet and handed it to the man. Despite her unhappiness with him, his generosity touched her.

They entered a darkened foyer that opened to a large, rectangular room. A single battery-powered lantern sat on a bookcase, casting shadows onto scarred plaster walls and illuminating a dozen or so cots. Several were occupied by sleeping figures, many of which were women and children.

Chase led Lily down another hall and into a second, smaller room. In the darkness he found two folded cots in the far corner and proceeded to unfold and set them up.

Lily knew they wouldn't be safe here for long. But she'd never been so glad to see a cot in her life. Her back ached with increasing intensity, telling her she needed to get off her feet, at least for a little while.

"You look dead exhausted."

Bad word choice, she thought. Chase had unfolded a single blanket and set a thin pillow on the cot. For her, she realized. "I'm pregnant, not sick."

"You need to rest while you can."

"It's hard to relax knowing men with guns are out there wanting to kill me."

"I'm not going to let anything happen to you." He patted the cot. "Come on, Lily. I'm worried about you. You're pale. Lie down for a few minutes."

Under any other circumstances Lily would have refused. She didn't want to be here. Didn't want to be with him. She wanted to go home where she would be safe and the world was predictable. But she could no longer ignore the ache in her back. She'd been on her feet far too long. At this stage of her pregnancy, she didn't want to push her luck.

"What about you?" she asked, her gaze flicking to the bloodstain on his shirt. In the darkness it appeared black.

"I'm fine."

"It's a bullet wound, isn't it?"

"It's a graze."

She shook her head, disbelieving he could be so flippant about something as serious as a gunshot wound. "God, this is *so* you, Chase."

"I'll take care of it as soon as we're safe."

"And when will that be?"

Grimacing, he lowered his eyes, but only for a moment. "Have you eaten?"

Back at the hospital, she'd been famished, but the terror and adrenaline had stolen her appetite. "No, but I'm not hungry."

"There's a soup kitchen in the back," he said. "Let me see if I can rouse a volunteer and get you something to eat."

Too tired to argue, Lily sat on the cot.

Before she realized what he was going to do, Chase leaned close and lifted her feet onto the thin mattress. "Lie down." One side of his mouth curved. "Might be your last chance for a while."

She looked at him as he leaned his tall, sinewy frame over her, his long, unruly hair framing his face. She couldn't see it in the dark, but she recalled the jagged white scar above his left eye. He looked even better than she remembered.

His voice sounded so sincere, so concerned, she did as he said. The moment she stretched out, all the adrenaline that had fueled her for the past seventeen hours ebbed. Her muscles went slack as exhaustion staked its claim on her body. She didn't want Chase to leave her, but she'd rather cut off her right hand than admit he made her feel safe.

He must have noticed her uneasiness, because he hung back. "You'll be all right here, Lily."

The way he said it almost made her believe it. Almost. But almost wasn't good enough. "It's not just me I have to worry about now."

She felt his gaze drill into her with an intensity that left her breathless. "At some point we're going to have to talk about that."

Not now, was all she could think. She was too exhausted to face his questions and the truth she'd hidden for seven-and-a-half months. It wasn't going to be a pleasant conversation. Lily had decided the moment she'd found out she was pregnant that she would never let Chase Vickers know his child.

Chapter Three

Aidan Shea couldn't believe they'd gotten away. He'd been so close he could smell Vickers's fear. He could see the terror white on the woman's face. He'd reveled in both, and hoped he could make good on all the things he had planned for them.

So far, those carefully laid plans had done nothing but blow up in his face.

He'd been meticulous in building his strategy. Months of planning and hundreds of hours of work had gone into this operation. He'd paid tens of thousands of dollars for the explosives blueprint. He'd dealt with men he wouldn't turn his back on, lest he risk a knife between his ribs. He'd spent six months building two utterly flawless bombs—devices powerful enough to take out both power plants in the city and inflict enough damage so that it would be days before electricity was restored.

Every aspect of the operation had been analyzed to the last detail, every variable countered with a constant. Every second had been synchronized so that the timing was perfect.

What the hell had gone wrong?

The question nagged like a migraine. But Aidan knew the answer. Chase Vickers was what had gone wrong. Evidently, the son of a bitch had nine lives and the luck of a gambler. Aidan had heard the man was good. Still, he'd underestimated him. He wouldn't make the same mistake twice.

Disappointment ate at him, but he wasn't unduly worried. Not yet, anyway. The game was still in its early stages. And he was, after all, a driven man—and with good reason. This mission was his life's work. He had an old score to settle—for himself and his father. Come hell or high water, he would see it through to the end.

The cell phone clipped to his belt vibrated. Glancing at the display window, he smiled and hit Talk.

"Did you get the woman?" He recognized the voice on the other end. His father. Liam Shea.

"She escaped."

"How did that happen?"

"Vickers showed up."

"Interesting development."

"I thought so."

"Watch him. He's very good at what he does."

"Yeah, well, so am I."

A tense silence ensued, then Liam asked. "Where are they now?"

"Somewhere in Chinatown," Aidan replied.

"I don't like this. You need to find them. If you have to, kill the woman now. She's expendable."

"With all due respect, I think that would be premature at this point. She's our ace in the hole."

"I'm willing to sacrifice her to get my hands on Vickers. I want that son of a bitch on his knees and begging when I put a bullet in his brain."

"Rest assured, he'll beg. If not for his own life, for hers." Aidan thought of the woman's condition and smiled. "She's pregnant."

"His?"

"The timing is right."

"No matter. He's weak when it comes to women. The child's parentage won't matter. When we kill her, it will have even more impact." He made a sound low in his throat. "What about the other part of the mission?"

The bomb, Aidan thought, and smiled. He'd planted the high-power explosives himself in a very central location that would have a maximum impact of terror on the good citizens of Boston.

"Done," he said.

"Excellent." Liam Shea sighed. "I've waited a long time for this."

"It won't be long now."

"Let's stick to the plan as closely as possible, but if you have to divert to get the job done, do it."

"Understood."

"Find them, Aidan." Urgency laced his father's voice.

"I've got two of our best men on it. They're like bloodhounds. I'm certain Vickers and the bitch are here in China-town. I've got a couple of snitches with sharp eyes. I'll ask around. Rest assured, we'll find them."

"Let me know the instant you do. I want to be smiling when Vickers dies."

"Wouldn't have it any other way." Breaking the connection, Aidan clipped the phone to his belt and set out to find Vickers and the pregnant woman.

"LILY."

Chase placed the paper plate of crackers, cheese and fruit on the beat-up table next to the cot where she lay sleeping. He'd been gone only a few minutes, but already she was out cold, a sure sign of complete physical exhaustion.

Taking in the pale cast of her complex-ion, he felt a quick and savage twinge of guilt. Intellectually he knew this wasn't his fault. Not directly, anyway. But he'd always known his work with Eclipse might catch up with him one day. He'd known it could place the people he cared about at risk. It was one of the reasons he avoided close relationships.

But those dangers hadn't been enough to keep him from his work. It sure as hell hadn't been enough to keep him from getting involved with Lily.

Lowering himself onto the cot next to hers, he put his elbows on his knees and rubbed at the ache behind his eyes. "What a mess," he muttered.

Remembering the cell phone he'd commandeered from the Asian man, he pulled it from his pocket and again dialed his half brother, Shane Peters. When it went to voice mail, he left another message and dialed Ty's number. Another layer of uneasiness washed over him when Ty didn't answer. It was unusual for either man not to answer. What the hell was going on?

Chase forced his mind back to the ambush in the limo and tried to think of who might be responsible and why. A frightening number of faces and names came to mind. Vicious men he'd played a role in bringing to justice. Had one of them targeted Lily in the name of revenge? If so, who had the resources for such a well-orchestrated attack?

Chase racked his brain, but time and time again he found his eyes straying to the woman a few feet away. In the shimmering yellow light of the battery-powered lantern, her face looked angelic. She lay curled on her side with both hands tucked beneath her pillow. Her knees were drawn up slightly. She was so beautiful it hurt just to look at her. The pain twisted like a dull knife between his ribs.

He could just make out the soft curves of her full breasts and the bulge of her belly. The reality that she was pregnant hit him like a sledgehammer. He couldn't get that out of his mind. He still couldn't quite believe it.

"Why didn't you tell me?" he whispered.

But Chase knew why. She'd never approved of his penchant for risk taking, the secret work that took him away and sent him home battered and bruised. In the past he'd always written off her lack of support as a lack of understanding, or an overreaction based on emotion. Now that he'd brought danger into her life, he knew he'd been wrong. He'd placed her baby— *his* baby—in jeopardy. The only question that remained was how he was going to keep them safe and make things right.

Chase didn't have a clue.

He'd been half in love with Lily Garrett from the moment he'd laid eyes on her three years ago. She was everything he was not, his polar opposite in every way. While he liked being on the road, bouncing from one city to another, one foreign country to the next, she tended to be a homebody. She preferred routine and familiarity. He thrived on danger and living life by the seat of his pants. She had a level head. He was as reckless as a storm-tossed sea.

He'd always believed those contrasts were one of the reasons they'd been drawn to each other with such power and passion. While that was true in many ways, those stark differences were also what had ultimately torn them apart. The truth of that hurt more than he wanted to admit.

Raised in a series of foster homes since the age of ten, Chase had never known the familiarity and comfort of family. The series of families who'd raised him had been virtual strangers—and they'd treated him as such. He'd grown up alone with a chip on his shoulder and no close ties. Then he met Lily and for the first time in his life he knew what it was like to connect with another human being.

He met her when a mission left him with a broken arm. His brother had taken him to the New England Medical Center emergency room. While Chase sat on the gurney, Lily walked in and began treating him. He hadn't been able to take his eyes off her. He liked to laugh about it now, but he'd always secretly thought that was the night he'd fallen in love with her.

It took six tries in the following weeks, but he'd finally convinced her to go out with him. Once she did, his fate was sealed. She was the only pure and innocent thing in his life, and he'd always looked upon her with a sort of reverence. She was like a long, deep breath of fresh air after weeks of stagnant city smog. A month into their relationship he'd invited her to his cabin home on the jagged Maine coast. He'd taken her for a ride on his speedboat. She'd asked him to slow down; he'd gone faster. That night, they'd made love for the first time. The experience had rocked his world. That was when Chase realized he was in over his head. Him. Mr. Independent. Mr. Love 'em and Leave 'em. Lily, the levelheaded emergency room nurse who thrived on all that was normal in the world, had become the center of his.

Over the next few months, he saw her as much as he could between missions. But after the first year or so, the injuries he sustained while on missions, his disappearing for weeks at a time without a word, began to take a heavy toll on their relationship. Finally, when he came back from North Africa with a closed head injury, Lily had asked him to choose: her or his work. Instead of listening with his heart, Chase had listened with his ego. In the end she'd walked away, and like the ass he was, he'd let her go.

It was the beginning of the end.

For months, he'd assured himself he'd done the right thing. He didn't want a woman telling him what to do or how to live his life. During that time, his tactics during missions became increasingly reckless. He volunteered for the most dangerous assignments. Assignments most sane men did their best to steer clear of. It was almost as if he were tempting fate to take a swipe at him. Then a shattered femur laid him up for several weeks. Alone in his cabin with nothing but time to think about his life—about Lily and all he'd lost—he realized how foolish he'd been for letting her go.

With his leg in a cast, he'd driven from Maine to Boston and gone directly to her apartment. There had been no romance or flowers or even a candlelit dinner. One look, one kiss, and he'd taken her down on the floor, where they'd made desperate, passionate love. Afterward, realizing what he'd done, Chase left before daylight. That had been seven and a half months ago, and he hadn't seen Lily since.

Until tonight.

As he looked at her sleeping form, a yearning for something profound but elusive tugged hard at him. The only time he felt whole was when he'd been with Lily. He'd tried to find fulfillment elsewhere by throwing himself into his work. But he hadn't succeeded. Now she was in danger, his baby was in danger, and it was his fault.

"Vickers, you're an idiot," he muttered into the darkness.

Sighing, Chase pulled the cell phone from his pocket and checked his service. Three bars. Why, then, weren't Shane or Ty calling him back?

Undeterred, he called the only other person he could think of: Ben Parker, an FBI agent stationed in the Boston area, whom he'd met several months ago through Shane.

Ben picked up on the first ring with a curt utterance of his name.

"Are you the only person in this friggin' town who answers his phone?" Chase asked.

"Busy night, bro."

"What's going on?"

"You mean aside from all hell breaking loose?" Ben's laugh was strained. "Someone tried to get to Shane tonight."

Chase closed his eyes. "He okay?"

"Narrow escape, but he's fine."

Relief swept through him with such force that for a moment he couldn't speak.

"You there?" Ben asked.

"Yeah." But his mind was reeling. That he had been ambushed just an hour ago was no coincidence.

Concern trickled through Chase as dark possibilities rose like a storm inside him. "They tried to get to me, too, Ben."

The other man's curse burned through the line. "You in one piece?"

"I'm fine."

"You able to ID them?"

"There was something familiar about one of the men, but I'm certain I've never seen him before."

"How did it happen?"

Chase described the ambush. Thinking of his limo, he frowned. "Wrecked Irma."

"Hopefully the looters won't get her."

"Thanks for planting that thought." His next statement made the hairs on the back of his neck prickle. "Ben, they tried to kill Lily."

"Lily Garrett? The nurse you—"

"That's the one," Chase interjected, not wanting him to finish the sentence.

"Damn. Is she all right?"

"She's with me."

"Good. Keep her with you. I don't have to tell you these bastards mean business."

Chase glanced down at the graze on his arm where the pain was coming to life. "No, you don't."

"If they tried to get to Lily, that means they tailed you. They researched her."

"If they were able to tail me without me noticing, they're probably professionals. They've probably got some connections."

The other man fell silent. Tension traveled through the line. Chase got a bad feeling in the pit of his stomach. "Any idea who might be behind this?"

"Not yet, but we've got people on it," Ben said after a moment. "I don't know if this ties in, but the vice president has been kidnapped."

"I heard." He got that prickly sensation again. "Vice President Davis was at the black-tie affair where I picked up the client who ambushed me. There's got to be a connection."

"We're trying to figure out what it is."

"You think the blackout is part of this?"

"I hope not, but we're not ruling out anything at this point. We've got BP&L crews working on both power stations."

"I didn't realize there were two plants."

"One in Charlestown, across the river, and the other in South Boston."

"You think it was sabotage?"

A pause ensued. "We've had unsubstantiated reports of simultaneous explosions, but nothing has been verified as of yet. Because of the power outage, communication has been hit or miss." He paused. "We're vulnerable, Chase. And prime for another attack."

The news struck him like a ton of bricks. Chase almost couldn't believe it. His mind scrolled through possible explanations. Random terrorism from some fanatical group. The kidnapping of the vice president by some homegrown political nutcase. But when you threw in synchronized ambushes on him and his brother, he knew there was another possibility that hit much closer to home.

The actions were connected, intentional—and aimed directly at a select group. A group from the past.

"Do you want to come in?" Ben asked him. "I can set you and Lily up in a safe house."

The thought appealed, but only because of Lily. Chase much preferred the freedom to move independently. But if the ambush was part of a conspiracy that reached all the way to the vice president, chances were the thugs had inside help. The FBI couldn't necessarily keep her safer than he could.

"No," he said. "We're safe for now."

"Where are you?"

Silence roared for an instant. Chase knew it was crazy not to trust Ben Parker, but his instincts told him not to answer. "Not over an open line, Ben."

"No problem. But, Chase, let me know if you want to bring her in."

"I'm not going to let anything happen to her," he insisted.

"If anything develops, I'll let you know."

At that the two men disconnected, and Chase was left alone with his thoughts, a woman he had once loved more than life itself, and a terrible fear that he might not be able to keep his word.

LILY JERKED AWAKE, her heart pounding. For a moment she was disoriented and didn't know where she was. Then the memory of everything that had happened rushed over her in a torrent. The blackout. The man with the gun. The ambush at the hospital. Chase's hand over hers as he shepherded her away from the danger.

Chase.

Struggling to a sitting position, she looked around to find the other cot vacant. Where was he? On the table next to her sat a plate heaped with crackers, cheese and some fruit. That he'd thought to bring her food shouldn't have touched her, but it did.

Chase had always affected her that way. She saw the good in him above all else. She saw his flaws and human imperfections only when confronted with them.

He was the only man she'd ever met who could make her act first and consider the consequences later. A cautious person by nature, Lily had never understood her reaction to him. It scared her almost as much as the power of her feelings for him.

She knew he cared. As much as he could, anyway. His background explained some of the reasons he was unable to give her the stability she needed. Chase didn't talk about it much, but one rainy night, lying in her bed, he told her about his childhood. He told her about his father disappearing without so much as an explanation when he was just a boy. He told her about his mother dying when he was only ten years old. About his half brother, Shane, going off to college and leaving him to the foster care system. A system that hadn't worked for an angry kid full of resentment and pain.

The truth of the matter was she cared for him. Too damn much if she wanted to be honest about it. But there was no way she would let her feelings for Chase dictate her life. Not ever again.

The baby chose that moment to kick, driving home the knowledge that there was no place in her world for the kind of dangers Chase presented. She had no desire to live her life wondering when, or if, he would return home from one of his secret missions.

It crossed her mind that now was probably a good time to steal away. But even though he represented all the things she didn't want in her life, deep inside she knew if anyone could keep her safe in the face of danger, it was Chase Vickers.

In a physical sense, anyway. Lily wasn't so sure about her heart. Despite her efforts to free herself from him and everything he represented, something profound remained between them. A special bond she hadn't been able to sever no matter how hard she tried. A link she could try to deny until forever. But she knew that no matter what happened, there would always be a special place for him in her heart.

Her weakness for him only proved she'd done the right thing by walking away. Once electricity was restored to the city and the gunmen were caught, she planned to walk away again.

But in the darkness of the homeless shelter, knowing there were men with guns who meant her harm, that knowledge was little comfort.

Setting her hand on her abdomen, she swung her legs over the side of the cot and struggled to her feet. The ache in her back had eased, but only marginally. The most pressing matter, however, was her need for the ladies' room, the bane of her pregnancy.

Taking a final look at the empty cot, she moved down the darkened hall toward the main room. Beds filled with sleeping bodies lined the walls. Several privacy dividers had been set up. Relief slid through her when, in the glow of battery-powered lanterns, she saw the Restroom sign at the far end of the room.

The ladies' room stood in near darkness, the only illumination coming from a battery-powered night light. Quickly she took care of business, then washed her face and hands. She was midway down the hall when the shuffle of shoes just beyond in the main room stopped her cold. She wanted to think it was Chase, looking for her, but inexplicably, her heart began to pound.

On impulse, Lily stopped and pressed her back to the wall. Peering around the corner, she saw the silhouettes of two men. Muffled voices reached her. But it was the sight of the gun that sent her heart into her throat.

All she could think was that they'd found her. But how? She couldn't imagine anyone getting the drop on Chase. Then again she'd never imagined an ambush at the hospital, either. She wanted desperately to find him, warn him, but there was no chance of doing so without being seen. All she could do was hide and hope they didn't find her.

Slinking back into the hallway, Lily cradled her abdomen and tried to think. Beyond, the hall continued past the main room to a rear exit. Could she make it to the door without being spotted, then get back inside to warn Chase?

She peeked around the corner again. The men separated, one walking toward the front of the room, the other starting toward her. Lily's heart leaped into a hard staccato, and her pulse pounded like a freight train in her ears. Oh dear God, he was coming her way, and she was trapped.

She looked around wildly. In the dim light she spotted a second door midway to the exit. Twenty feet separated her from the man. Knowing it was now or never, she ducked low and darted toward the door, praying it was unlocked.

She twisted the knob and shoved. Relief made her legs go weak when the door opened. The room was nearly pitch-black, lit only by a slant of pre-dawn light filtering in through the single window. Blindly, Lily felt her way along the wall. Her thigh bumped into something solid. Eyes wide, she reached out and ran her hands over the piece of furniture. A desk, she realized.

Footfalls sounded outside the door. Struggling to control her breathing, Lily sidled around the desk and bumped into a chair. The sound seemed thunderous in the small room. Had he heard her? Pushing the chair back, she knelt and crawled beneath the desk. She was in the process of pulling the chair into the kneehole when the door swung open.

Lily stopped breathing. Her heart pounded so loud she feared it might give away her position. Squeezing her eyes closed, she put her hand over her mouth to stifle the scream creeping up her throat. She could hear her breaths rushing through her nose and prayed the man with the gun didn't hear her.

Seconds passed like hours. Light slashed through the darkness, and she realized the man had a flashlight. The only thing separating her from certain discovery was the desk's modesty panel. The beam swept left and right. Lily glanced at the floor, saw the toes of wing-tip shoes inches from where she crouched. He stood less than a foot away from her, so close she could hear him breathing.

After what seemed like an eternity, he

cursed and stepped back. She heard his shoes shuffle against the floor. The beam made a final sweep of the room then winked out behind the closing door.

Relief brought tears to her eyes, but she didn't make a sound. She remained unmoving for several minutes. When she could stand it no longer, she silently pushed the chair from the kneehole and crawled out. Her legs tingled from lack of circulation, but she barely noticed the discomfort. She was just glad to be alive.

Intent on finding Chase to warn him, she tiptoed to the door and opened it an inch. Two inches. She peered into the hall, relief sliding through her when she found it empty. Silently closing the door, she pressed her back to it and tried to get a grip on the fear. Had the men gone? Was it safe to venture from the room? Where was Chase?

She'd decided to wait a few more minutes just to be sure the man was gone when suddenly the doorknob squeaked. She darted back, paralyzed with terror as the door swung open. Horror swept through her at the sight of the gunman.

His face was a pale oval in the darkness. She saw the pistol in his right hand, the flashlight in his left.

"You think I'm stupid?" he snarled.

A scream poured from her throat. Lily turned to run, but in the tiny office, there was no place to go. She was trapped with a monster bent on killing her. Looking around for a weapon, anything she could use to protect herself, she spied the letter opener on the desk and snatched it up.

"Get away from me!" she screamed.

The gun came up. Realizing she couldn't get close enough to use the letter opener, she threw it with all her might, hoping to strike him in the face. But he deflected it, and the letter opener clattered to the floor.

"Stop or I'll put a hole in you," he said.

Lily sprinted toward the window. Behind her, a gunshot exploded. Willing to risk getting cut to pieces as opposed to facing the gunman, she set her hand against her abdomen and hurled herself through the glass.

Chapter Four

From the men's room, Chase heard the gunshot. The sons of bitches had found them. Found Lily. Terror like he'd never felt before slammed into him at the thought of her being hurt—or worse.

All because of you, hotshot.

"Not gonna happen," he ground out.

A split second and he was out the door, rushing down the hall. In the semidarkness he saw the office door ajar. It had been closed when he'd walked by just a few minutes earlier.

The sound of shattering glass exploded. Beyond the point of considering his own safety, he burst into the room. A man stood with his back to the door, looking out a broken window, a pistol in his right hand.

Fury overtook Chase. He didn't think, didn't hesitate. He charged. The man spun just as Chase struck him with the full force of his body weight, slamming him against the wall. Breath rushed from the man's lungs in an animalistic roar.

Chase caught a glimpse of the gun. Rage that this bastard would hurt a pregnant woman—*his* woman—sent his fist flying. His knuckles crashed into the man's cheek, and Chase heard bone crunching. Pain shot from his hand to his elbow, but he was too enraged to pay it any mind. Even as he drew back a second time, all he could think of was Lily. Had she been shot? Cut by glass from the broken window?

The next thing Chase knew, the man was lying on the floor, unconscious. Through the window he saw Lily, and his heart raged in his chest. Oh dear God, let her be all right, he prayed. Quickly, he stooped and snatched up the man's pistol and shoved it into the waistband of his slacks. He yanked the man's wallet from his pocket, dropped it into his own. Next came the cell phone, which he clipped onto his belt.

Movement at the door arrested his attention. Chase spun, brought up the gun. His arm shook when he took aim, expecting another gunman. But it was only the man who ran the shelter.

The man's mouth opened but no sound emerged.

"Sorry, old man." Chase lowered the gun. "Thought you were someone else."

The old man gestured toward the broken window and scolded him in Chinese.

"Tell it to the cops," he said, and slipped through the window.

The window faced the mouth of an alley on the north side of the building. Lily stood a few feet away, her back pressed against the dirty brick as if she were no longer capable of standing on her own power. Her face was so white, she looked like a ghost. All Chase could think was that she'd been shot.

"Lily, are you all right?"

He didn't wait for an answer. Striding toward her, he set his hands on her shoulders. "Lily."

"I'm...okay."

He tried to touch her, but she slapped his hand away. "Don't."

"You're pale as hell."

"That animal in there tried to kill me."

"Calm down, honey. I just need to make sure you're all right." Clenching his jaw against the remnants of anger, of fear, he ran his shaking hands quickly over her for a cursory physical assessment. His heart tumbled into his stomach when his left hand came away red.

"My God, you're bleeding." His stomach plunged. "Where are you—" He thought of the baby, and the earth seemed to wobble beneath his feet. Dear God, if he'd caused her to go into early labor…

"Chase."

He barely heard her utter his name. He was too intent on the blood. Her blood. On his hands. The symbolism was almost too much to take.

"Chase."

Something in her voice snapped him out of it. He glanced over his shoulder to see two men with guns sprint past the mouth of the alley just thirty feet away. No time to rest or assess her injury.

"It's not the baby," she said. "I'm cut."

"Where?"

"My thigh. It happened when I went through the window."

A weird sense of relief rippled through him. Simultaneously, inappropriate thoughts of her thighs crowded his mind, but Chase quickly banked them. "You must have been terrified to risk going through that glass."

"He would have killed me if I hadn't." Placing a protective hand over her abdomen, she looked away.

Guilt churned hot and jagged inside him. He hated it that she'd been hurt. That she could have been killed. Why the hell did these violent men have to involve her?

"I'm not the only one bleeding," she said.

Chase looked into her eyes. The beauty of her face made him ache deep inside, nudged the fear he'd felt earlier to the back of his mind. More than anything he wanted to hold her. He wanted to touch her and make sure she wasn't seriously injured.

For the moment he had to settle for keeping her safe.

"It'll keep." He grasped her hand. "We have to go."

He took her to the opposite end of the alley. Cars and several groups of people crowded the street. Some of the Chinese vendors had set up tea lights at their doorways where they congregated, no doubt guarding against vandals and looters.

Looking both ways, Chase turned south and pulled Lily into an easy run. Easy for him, anyway. He could only imagine how physically grueling this was for her. His mind spun through possible hiding places.

Next to him, he could feel her lagging. Worry nipped at his conscience. At the end of the block, he slowed to a jog and cast her a look.

He checked both directions. "This way."

Sticking to the shadows beneath the many storefront canopies, he walked briskly, tugging Lily along behind him.

"Where are we going?" she asked breathlessly.

"A place where we can disappear for a little while."

As they approached Atlantic Avenue, the darkened shadow of the forty-one-story South Station Tower loomed over them like some behemoth beast. Beyond, Chase could just make out the ornate granite facade of the century-old South Station bus and rail terminal.

It was the perfect place for two people to get lost in the crowd. Hordes of weary travelers ebbed and flowed on the wide walkway in front of the building. The old-fashioned streetlamps stood dark, making it difficult to see individual faces, a plus in this case.

"If we go in there and we're followed, we'll be trapped," Lily said, eyeing the place.

Chase stopped and set his hands on her shoulders. She was so small and soft. She felt fragile beneath his hands, though he knew Lily Garrett was anything but. Still, she was pregnant and injured; there was no way they could continue without rest.

"I've still got a few cards up my sleeve," he said.

She searched his face. "You always do, don't you?"

The words were more accusation than observation. Not wanting to go there, he put his arm around her shoulders and guided her through the arched doorway and into the throngs of disgruntled rail and bus passengers. Inside the great room, the station management had set up generator-powered lighting.

Chase ushered her to the bank of elevators. He'd known the cars wouldn't be operational because of the blackout, but he was still bummed. "Damn."

"Where are we going?"

"I studied a map of this place once during a mission a few years back. If I can get us into the underground level and find the right door, I think there's a place where we can lay low for a while."

"What about security?"

"Give me some credit, will you?"

Standing there with her lips pulled into a frown, her eyes level on his, she didn't look impressed.

"Look, this place is over a hundred years

old," he said. "There's a tunnel that was begun but only partially completed during the renovation back in the seventies. There's no rail service, of course, but the room is tiled and ventilated. If I can remember how to get there and find the right door, I can pick the lock and we're in."

"You make breaking into one of the most secure ground transportation hubs in the country sound easy."

"Honey, you have no idea."

"Probably a good thing at this point."

They walked the perimeter of the great room. On the north wall, Chase found an unlit stairwell sign. Turning, he quickly scanned the crowd, looking for men with guns, a face he recognized, someone paying too much attention to them, but he saw nothing out of the ordinary.

Shoving open the door, he took Lily's hand and they descended into the blackness.

LILY HAD NEVER SEEN such darkness. Even though Chase was close enough to touch, she couldn't see his face. She couldn't so much as see a single shadow. She couldn't even see her hand when she held it mere inches from her eyes.

As they descended the stairs, claustrophobia closed over her like a giant, smothering hand. The air grew cooler. Only Chase's hand felt incredibly warm and reassuring as it gripped hers.

Abruptly, a light flicked on. She glanced over, realized he'd pilfered the gunman's flashlight back at the shelter. Relief made her sigh.

"You okay?" he asked.

Not wanting him to know just how close she was to the end of her endurance, she forced a smile. "Just feeling a little claustrophobic."

"Light should help. I'm hoping the auxiliary lighting is on in the room I'm looking for."

They came to a steel door painted utilitarian blue. Chase tried the knob, but it was locked.

"Like that's a surprise," Lily said. "What do we do now?"

"Pick the lock."

"Of course we do."

Giving her a half smile, he passed her the flashlight. "Hold this."

Lily took the small light, wondering how long the batteries would last. She shone the beam on the lock. Beside her, Chase reached into his rear pocket and pulled out what looked like a wallet. When he opened it, an array of shiny tools came into view. A lock-picking kit, she realized, and shook her head. "Don't tell me you carry that around with you."

"Never leave home without it." Touching her arm, he pushed the beam toward the lock. "Two minutes and we'll be snug inside."

Snug wasn't the word that came to mind, but Lily was in desperate need of some downtime. She was in good physical condition. So far she'd had a relatively easy pregnancy. But in the past couple of weeks, late-term discomforts had set in. Combined with the trauma of the night, stress, too much activity and too little sleep, she felt lucky to be standing at all.

Kneeling, Chase went to work on the

lock. Lily watched, amazed by the deftness of his hands, the speed and surety with which he worked. Around her, she could hear the low rumble of something she imagined was a generator. Somewhere, another type of machinery buzzed. Farther away, water dripped.

An audible *click* interrupted her thoughts. Relief went through her when the door squeaked open.

Chase usurped the flashlight from her and ushered her inside as if he were a doorman at some five-star hotel. "Home sweet home."

The room was small and rectangular with a gray tile floor and matching walls. It held a table and chairs, a vending machine and a humming refrigerator. On the far wall was a utility closet.

"Have a seat."

She startled at the sound of his voice.

"Easy," he said. "We're safe for now."

But the reason she'd jumped had nothing to do with the gunmen and everything to do with the man she now found herself alone with.

He leaned against the doorjamb,

watching her with an intensity that immediately unnerved her. "You okay?"

"Fine." Annoyed with herself for letting
him get to her on a level she didn't like,
Lily sat down. The instant her body made
contact with the seat, she felt herself
melting with exhaustion.

"Let me see if I can find us some light,
so I can see to that cut on your leg."

Too tired to argue, too tired to even
move, Lily watched him cross to the utility
closet and open the door. "Here we go.
Let's see if this works."

Overhead, a single fluorescent bulb
buzzed, then dim light poured down on
them. "All the comforts of home," he said.

"Not quite," she called out.

He stuck his head out and grinned. "I'm
not finished yet."

She could hear him rummaging around
and tried not to smile. Damn him for
charming her when she didn't want to be
charmed.

"Let's see," he said from the closet.
"We've got a mop. Push broom. Air
freshener."

"What? No guns or bombs?"

"This ought to do the trick." He stepped out of the closet, a dispenser of antibacterial soap in one hand, a small, portable shop light in the other, and a towel slung over his shoulder.

"Must be our lucky day," she said dryly.

"Battery-powered shop light to the rescue." Glancing up, he stepped onto one of the chairs and hooked the light onto a darkened overhead fixture. He flipped it on and bright light rained down. "Like I said, all the comforts of home."

"If you don't mind living in a cave."

His eyes were sober when they landed on Lily. "I need to take a look at that cut, then I'll let you get some rest."

"I'm a nurse and perfectly capable of—"

"Let me do this." As if realizing his harsh tone, he glanced away, his expression softening. "I need to make sure you're all right."

The cut on her leg was the last thing that worried Lily. Exhaustion and the now constant pain in her lower back overshadowed the sting of the wound. But Lily knew there was more to her resistance than the minor nature of the cut. As a nurse, she knew even a shallow gash could become infected if left untreated. But in order for Chase to administer first aid, he would have to touch her. He would have to put his hands on her thigh.

That kind of closeness was the last thing Lily needed to contend with. As much as she didn't want to admit it, every time Chase touched her something seemed to short-circuit in her brain. The last time, they'd ended up naked on the floor of her apartment.

Stopping the errant thoughts cold, she sighed. That was the past, she reminded herself. She'd loved him once, but no more. Lily had her baby to think of now.

"Nothing personal, Lily, but you're going to have to lose the pants."

His voiced jerked her from her reverie. Lily looked up to see Chase standing over her, a small pail in one hand, a soap dispenser and roll of paper towels in the other.

She stared at him, his words ringing in her head like the lyrics of some annoying song. "Not in this lifetime," she heard herself say.

"Maybe this will help..." Never taking his eyes from hers, Chase set the items on the table and proceeded to take off his shirt.

An alarm shot through Lily as the dark thatch of chest hair and a six-pack abdomen loomed into view. "Wh-what are you doing?"

"Protecting your modesty."

"By taking off your shirt?"

One side of his mouth quirked. "You can tie it around your waist, keep yourself covered."

"Oh." Her alarm subsided, but it was only a temporary reprieve. As he worked the shirt from his shoulders, her eyes took on a life of their own. She got the impression of hard-as-rock muscle and tried not to think of all the times he'd held her with those arms or all the times she'd run her fingers over his skin.

Then she spotted the wound just above his bicep and put her hand over her mouth.

"Oh, Chase. That's no graze. For God's sake, it looks bad."

He handed her his shirt. "Take off your pants or I'll take them off for you."

"Fine." Exasperated with him, with the situation, with herself, she yanked the shirt from his grasp. "Turn around."

He did as she asked.

Untying the drawstring waist, she stepped out of her scrub pants, then quickly wrapped his shirt around her bulging waist. "You can turn around."

She didn't miss the quick sweep of his gaze or the way his expression darkened when his eyes paused on her abdomen. He stared and for a moment she thought he would ask to touch her belly, but he didn't.

"Sit on the table," he said. "Put your feet on the chair."

Lily scooted onto the table and set both feet on the chair, careful to keep her panties and the tops of her thighs covered by his shirt. She knew it was silly to worry about something as trivial as modesty during a crisis, especially when she'd been intimate with this man on more than one occasion. But being pregnant and determined not to repeat the mistakes of her past, Lily had no intention of letting down her guard.

Without speaking, he approached, his attention focused on the cut. "Looks like you could have used a couple of stitches."

"Like I'm going to let you stick a needle in me."

He didn't smile. Instead, he settled into one of the chairs and reached for the pail of water and the soap dispenser. "I guess we'll just have to make do with a bandage."

Up until now, Lily hadn't gotten a good look at the cut. In relation to her other discomforts, the cut had barely rated on the pain scale. Judging from the stain on her pants, though, it had bled plenty. The wound looked deep, with the flesh laid open the width of her little finger.

"Think you can butterfly it?" she asked.

His gaze flicked to hers. "I'm an EMT. I think I can handle it."

He dipped the paper towel into the water, then dispensed a generous amount of soap onto it and pressed it against the cut. The soap stung, but it wasn't the pain that had Lily's heart beating double time. It was the sight of Chase's hand on her thigh.

"Sorry," he said. "I know it hurts."

What hurts, she thought, *was your inability to put your dangerous lifestyle aside for me, the woman you claimed to love.*

Water under the bridge, she reminded herself and concentrated on the sting. She clung to the small physical pain because it was so much easier to deal with than the truth of what had happened between them.

"It's clean." He reached for a roll of masking tape and a paper towel he'd neatly folded. "Now here comes the bandage."

Setting his hand on the underside of her thigh, he gripped it while applying the makeshift bandage with the other. "Going to hurt when I tighten this thing."

"It's okay," Lily heard herself say. But, looking at him, feeling the old emotions churn inside her, she felt certain nothing was ever going to be okay again.

Chapter Five

Chase leaned back in the chair and listened to the whisper-soft sound of Lily's breathing. After he bandaged the cut on her leg, he'd talked her into lying down. As usual, she'd protested. But she must have been exhausted, because the instant her head hit the towel he'd folded for her to use as a pillow, she'd gone out like a light.

He wished he could turn off his own mind as readily, but he couldn't. He should try to get some sleep, or at the very least, rest. But he was wound as tight as a man could be and not snap. He needed to know who was behind the attempt on Lily's life. On his life and Shane's. He needed to know if that same person was behind the kidnapping of Vice President Davis and if the incidents were related to the blackout or merely coincidence.

Chase had long ago decided such a thing didn't exist. So who was behind the actions?

He had made plenty of enemies over the years, many of whom were violent and powerful men. The Federal Bureau of Prisons kept him informed of recent parolees. Was it possible one had slipped through the cracks? Still, one question nagged at him. Why sabotage the Boston power plants to get at him?

In that instant, in some small corner of his mind, something pinged. Dread swept through him with the violence of a tidal wave when he recalled a threat that had been made against his Special Forces team some eleven years ago after a high-profile and ultimately disastrous Middle Eastern rescue mission.

Fifty-eight people, including U.S. Secretary of State Geoffrey Rollins, had been taken hostage in civil-war-torn Barik. The hostages, mostly engineers, teachers and missionaries, were being held in a densely populated downtown, in the basement of a closely guarded building. The world prayed for their safe release. After several failed rescue attempts, an elite team was assembled.

Under the leadership of Commander Tom Bradley, the coterie consisted of security expert Shane Peters, computer ace Ethan Matalon, demolitions man Ty Jones, tactical expert Grant Davis, electrical specialist Liam Shea, linguistics man Frederick LeBron, and Chase. They were charged with getting the hostages out alive.

But something had gone terribly wrong.

Bent on revenge against the sect holding the hostages, Liam Shea disobeyed direct orders. He acted impulsively, without waiting for the commander's signal to cut the power to the building, throwing off the timing of the rescue. Alerted to an assault, the captors released cyanide gas in the basement, leading to the deaths of three hostages, including Secretary of State Rollins.

In the end, Shea was court-martialed and sent to prison, effectively terminating the political career he dreamed of. Teammate Grant Davis, on the other hand, having been hailed a hero in the mission for saving Shea's life, parlayed his military career into the second seat in the White House.

Throughout the trial, Liam Shea had maintained his innocence and went to prison a very angry man. But not before threatening the lives of everyone involved.

Was Shea behind this? Chase thought. Had he been released from prison, or escaped?

Had he ambushed the other men from the mission as well?

LeBron, now the king of Beau Pays, was in his country, ensconced in the Alps, and Tom Bradley had passed away years ago. But Ethan lived here in Boston, the owner of a successful software company, and Ty was here as part of the vice president's detail. Chase's pulse pounded. He had to contact Ethan and Ty and warn them…if it wasn't already too late.

Tension coursing through his body, Chase rose and pulled out the two cell phones. Both glowed with the No Signal light. Cursing, he hit the call history on the phone he'd appropriated from the gunman back at the shelter, and checked the outgoing call history. He recognized the area codes—Seattle and Boston, mostly— but not the individual numbers. Same for the incoming calls. Frustrated, he turned off the phones to conserve the low batteries.

He needed to know if Shea had been released from prison. But in order to do that, he needed a phone signal. He wasn't going to find it in the basement of a century-old building.

That brought him back to the situation at hand—and Lily. The last thing he wanted to do was put her in any more danger than she already was. On the other hand, he wasn't going to solve this thing by hiding out. The men with guns were not going to go away. Chase had to act, and he had to act now.

Scrubbing his hand over his face, he turned and, for the dozenth time, found his eyes on Lily. She lay on her side on a small rug with a folded towel tucked beneath her head. Her eyes were closed, her lashes dark and velvety against the pale skin of her face. Her knees were drawn up as far as her swollen belly would allow, as if she were trying to protect her unborn child even in sleep. She looked incredibly small and vulnerable lying there, and a fierce need to protect her rose up inside him with surprising force.

Chase knew better than to indulge in the moment but, even pregnant and disheveled, she was by far the most beautiful woman he'd ever laid eyes on. They'd had something special once. A small part of him wanted to believe they could recapture that old magic. But he knew there was no way she would ever give him access to her heart again.

Not that he wanted it, Chase reminded himself. He was better off alone. No entanglements. No one to ask questions. No one to answer to. No one to endanger when things went wrong.

But you've already put her in the line of fire, a rude little voice reminded.

Tearing his eyes away from her, Chase strode to the door and yanked it open. The hall beyond stood dark and quiet. Behind him, Lily slept soundly. For a split second, he hesitated, then reminded himself that no one knew they were here. She would be safe for a few minutes. It was imperative that he get in touch with Ben Parker. He had to let him know Liam Shea could be behind not only the simultaneous ambushes, but the kidnapping of the vice president and the blackout as well. God only knows what else could be in the works.

Chase locked the door behind him and headed for the nearest stairwell. Pulling the phone from his pocket, he checked the signal display as he walked, hoping he wouldn't have to leave the lower level in order to get a fair number of bars. No such luck.

Cursing beneath his breath, he yanked open the stairwell door and started up the stairs, keeping his eye on the phone. Midway up the stairwell, the No Signal light went out. Quickly, he dialed Ben Parker's number.

Though it wasn't yet six in the morning, the other man answered on the first ring.

Chase wasted no time on niceties. "I think Liam Shea might be behind this."

"What? How do you know?"

"He fits the profile. He's an electrical expert. He's made threats against the people involved. There's a direct connection between him and the vice president. We were all part of a botched rescue mission in the Middle East eleven years ago. Shea is the only man I can think of good enough to pull off these simultaneous attacks. I need to know if he was recently released from prison."

"I'll get right on it."

On the other end of the line, Chase heard computer keys clicking. After a moment, Parker asked, "Where are you?"

Chase didn't want to tell him. Not on this phone. But with Lily in tow, he didn't have a choice. He could no longer handle this alone. "I'm at South Station. I need for someone to pick us up. We're coming in."

"Is Lily Garrett still with you?"

"Yeah." Thinking of her pregnancy, Chase sat down on the stairwell step and closed his eyes. "She's seven-and-a-half months pregnant."

The short silence that followed told him

Ben Parker suspected Chase was the father. "All right. Stay put. I'll have someone there in twenty-five minutes. Where can they find you?"

"I'll find them." He terminated the call and dialed Ty's number but got voice mail. "Call me," he snapped, and left his number. Next he dialed Ethan.

The other man picked up on the second ring. "About time you called," Ethan began. "I'm sure you know by now all freaking hell has broken loose."

Relief swept through Chase at the sound of his friend's voice. "Yeah, and I think I know who—"

The blow came out of nowhere. One second he was sitting on the step, talking. The next he was laid out on the floor. Pain radiated from ear to ear, the world spun wildly. In the semidarkness, he sensed movement. The shuffle of shoes against the floor. He reached for his weapon, but a booted foot kicked it from his hand.

"We're going to hurt her," came a whispered voice. "She's going to die a slow, painful death. So is that baby of yours. All because of you."

Made furious by the words, Chase tried to rise, attempted to grab the other man's legs.

The second blow sent him spinning into darkness.

LILY WOKE to the golden glow of the battery-powered shop light. She lay on the small rug for a moment, getting her bearings, taking a mental inventory of her body. The backache was gone. The cut on her leg stung, but the pain was minimal. The most pressing issue was a full bladder and a grumbling tummy.

Stretching, feeling surprisingly rested, Lily sat up and looked around. "Chase?"

He was nowhere in sight. No surprise there. The man was like a phantom, appearing and disappearing without so much as a sound. She wondered if he'd gone for food. A glance at her watch told her she'd slept just over an hour. For now, the vending machine would have to do.

She rose, used the toilet in the utility closet, and washed her face and hands. She was midway to the vending machine and digging coins from her uniform pocket when a knock on the door sounded. Alarm filtered through her as she crossed to it. "Chase?"

"It's me. Open up."

Relief slid through her at the muffled voice. Twisting the lock, she pulled open the door. The next thing she knew a large man set his hand against her chest and shoved her back hard enough to make her stumble. Lily turned to run, but there was no place to go.

A scream tore from her throat. She darted to the utility closet and tried to slam the door, hoping that small space would buy her a few precious seconds. Time enough for Chase to reach them and put an end to this once and for all. But before she could slam it home, a booted foot was thrust inside.

"Not so fast," said a second man's voice.

She put her weight against the door, but she was no match for the two men on the other side. The door flew open, shoving her violently back. She struck the far wall hard enough to lose her breath. Two men entered the small room. They were young. One sported a goatee. Both wore long black coats and held ugly-looking pistols.

One of the men pulled the slide down on the gun, chambered a bullet and shifted the muzzle to her belly. "Now, pretty lady, excuse my rudeness, but you're going to do exactly as we say or I'll shoot that little one inside you. You got that?"

Terror swept through Lily with such force that she couldn't speak. She couldn't breathe. All she could think of was the baby.

Setting her hands over her belly, she nodded. "I'll do whatever you say," she said. "Please don't hurt my baby."

"Smart lady." The man grinned. "Here's what I want you to do."

CHASE WOKE to pain, waves of it crashing against his skull. Cold concrete ground into his cheek. Something warm tickled his temple. What the hell had happened?

A groan escaped him as he shifted. In the background, he heard metal clang against metal. He wanted to know where he was and how he'd gotten there, but he couldn't seem to open his eyes.

Then he remembered the ambush in the stairwell. The blow coming from behind. Another sending him into outer space. And Lily...

Thoughts of her sent him bolt upright. Pain tore through the back of his head, but he struggled to his feet anyway. Nausea seesawed in his gut, but Chase didn't have time to concentrate on the pain or give in to the sickness.

Darkness surrounded him. Whoever had ambushed him had taken his flashlight. But from the dim light filtering in through the tiny overhead window, he ascertained that he was still in the stairwell. Steel clanged again, and he realized the son of a bitch had handcuffed him to the pipe rail.

Bloody hell, how was he going to get out of this one?

A bigger question pushed into his mind when he remembered the man's whispered threats. *We're going to hurt her. She's going to die a slow, painful death. So is that baby of yours. All because of you.*

Panic gripped him. For several terrible seconds, Chase struggled like an animal, yanking against the handcuff, making sounds not even he could understand. He wanted to think it was the blow to his head that was causing him to act so irrationally. But he knew the reason went a hell of a lot deeper than that.

They were going to kill Lily. They were going to kill the baby.

"No!" he shouted in frustration.

Heart pounding, he went still and forced himself to calm down. The fuzziness in his head from being knocked unconscious slowly abated. His mind cleared. With his free hand, Chase felt around for the gun and phones, but they were gone. Cursing, he grappled for the lock-picking kit. It was the one thing the gunmen hadn't found.

He tugged the small kit from his pocket and went to work on the handcuff. Since his right hand was cuffed, he had to work left-handed. His vision had adjusted to the darkness, but Chase couldn't see well enough and had to feel his way through the process.

Sweat beaded on his forehead and ran down his back as he worked. All the while he tried not to imagine what the two gunmen would do to Lily when they found her.

We're going to hurt her. She's going to die a slow, painful death. So is that baby of yours. All because of you.

"Please, God, let her be all right," he whispered as he frantically worked to pick the lock.

A curse flew from his lips when his first attempt failed. His hands shook so violently he was screwing it up. *Easy does it,* whispered a small, calm part of his mind.

Closing his eyes briefly, Chase put Lily and all the terrible things that could happen to her out of his mind and focused on the lock. His heart rate slowed. His breathing evened out. His hands steadied.

Two minutes later the cuff clicked open. Chase's first instinct was to run directly to Lily and stop the men before they did something horrendous and irrevocable. But training and experience warned him rash actions would do nothing but get him shot.

Working frantically, he picked the other locked cuff and stuffed it into the pocket of his slacks. In the semidarkness, he searched the floor for anything that might have been left behind—a gun or phone—but he found nothing.

He needed a plan. He needed a weapon. A mode of communication with the outside world. The two gunmen could very well already have Lily in custody. There was no way he could rush in unarmed and get both of them out alive.

In his years with the military and with Eclipse, he'd found himself in worse situations. Still, this was different. This was personal. He'd never had to save the life of a woman he'd once loved, a woman he still cared for deeply. The woman who carried his child.

Chase took the steps two at a time to the top. Checking the small window in the door that led to the main hall, he slowly pushed it open and stepped out. Here the light was better. He started down the hall, trying each door he passed.

The first two doors were locked. The third

read Security. Chase didn't hesitate. Taking a deep breath, he shoved open the door.

An older man in a blue uniform sat at a desk. Four darkened monitors lined the wall ahead. He gave Chase a cop look when he walked in. "Can I help you?" he asked in a strong Boston accent.

"I want to report a crime." Putting his face in his hands, Chase moved closer to the desk.

"Calm down," the security guard said. "Tell me what happened."

With his face still in his hands, Chase collapsed into the chair and scooted closer. "They took my girlfriend. At gunpoint."

"Who?"

"I don't know." He inched closer. Almost there…

"They kidnapped her? At *gunpoint?*" The man reached for the radio. "Where did this happen?"

The instant the man turned away, Chase lunged and went for the gun. Eyes wide, gripping the radio like a weapon, the security officer tried to scramble back. "What the—"

A jab to the solar plexus silenced him.

When the man doubled over, Chase followed up with a chop to the base of his skull. The man sprawled on the floor.

"Sorry, old man." Glancing around, feeling the seconds tick by, Chase stuffed the gun into his waistband. He lifted an expandable baton from the man's belt, along with a flashlight and a cell phone. Pulling the cuffs from his own pocket, he snapped them onto the man's wrists. He found masking tape on the desk and peeled off enough to cover the man's mouth. Spotting a small supply closet at the back of the room, he dragged the man into it and locked the door.

Chase spent another minute searching the small office for anything he might be able to use. A locked cabinet snagged his attention. Safety-conscious law-enforcement types always kept the good stuff under lock and key. He quickly picked the lock, yanked open the cabinet. The cache of small arms and various riot gear didn't amount to much, but they would do in a pinch.

Armed with the .38 revolver, a concussion grenade, a canister of tear gas, and the resolve of a man facing his worst nightmare, he went in search of Lily.

Chapter Six

They were going to kill her.

That terrible fact jammed Lily's brain as the two men ushered her down the dark and narrow corridor. She was walking to her death. It was only a matter of time. The thought terrified her. But what really horrified her was the thought of her unborn child dying.

She wasn't above begging. She would do anything—*anything*—if she thought it would spare her baby's life. "I'll do whatever you want," she blurted out, her voice breathless with fear and adrenaline. "Please...just don't hurt my baby."

On either side of her, the men ignored her plea. They led her down the hall a few more feet, then stopped.

The man gripping her right bicep tightened his grip. "Elevator's out. Frickin' blackout. We gotta take the stairs."

The other man looked at Lily. "Where's Vickers?"

She stared into cold blue eyes that were as lifeless and cold as a Boston winter. "I don't know."

His gaze skimmed down the front of her. "If you want to save that kid, you'd better start talking, bitch."

He was a thickly built man with large facial features that made his head look too big for his body. "I swear to you," she said. "I honestly don't know. I was sleeping when he left. Probably to make a call."

"Who did he call?"

"I don't know."

The second man made a sound of frustration. He glared at Lily, and she saw cruelty in the depth of his gray eyes. "Lying bitch." He sneered at the other man. "She's yankin' your chain."

"I'm not," she choked.

Where are you, Chase? Please come.

They reached the door leading to the

stairs. The second man drew his weapon and shoved the door open. He looked up and down the stairwell, then motioned them in. "It's clear. Let's go."

The man with the blue eyes pushed her into the stairwell corridor, then addressed the other man. "Get on the horn and tell Eddie to meet us at the south exit."

The second man slid a sleek phone from his coat, punched numbers with a fat thumb. "We got the chick," he said. "No sign of Vickers. Yeah. Meet us at the south exit. Two minutes."

Frowning, he snapped the phone closed. "Let's get the hell outta here." Lips pulling back, he shoved Lily. "Time's a wastin', bitch. Hurry up and get up those stairs."

Numb with dread, Lily followed orders. Her heart beat so fast the rush of blood made her dizzy. She couldn't believe the situation had boiled down to this. That these two violent men would kill her and her child, and she would become just another Boston statistic.

She was midway to the landing when she heard a noise, as if something had fallen from above. An instant later an explosion rocked her brain. The man grasping her arm reeled backward, cursing. Lily fell to her hands and knees. Something metallic clanged behind her. She glanced over her shoulder in time to see smoke swirl from some type of steel canister.

"Gas!" shouted one of the men.

"Get the bitch!" said the other.

A scream tore from Lily's throat when he lunged at her. Acting on instinct, she slapped off his hand and scrambled on all fours up the remaining stairs.

At the top of the landing, Lily sucked in a breath, but it was like breathing in fire. Choking smoke filled the stairwell. The acrid gas entered her bronchial tubes like shards of molten glass. Her lungs seized. Clutching her belly, she doubled over and began to cough.

She screamed when strong arms gripped her from behind. All she could think was that she couldn't let the men take her back. Fighting for her life, she spun and tried to knee him. But her attacker danced aside.

"Get away from me!" she choked.

"Lily. Whoa. It's me, Chase. Settle down."

In the semidarkness and swirling smoke, she couldn't see his face. But she knew his voice. His touch. Relief washed over her with such power that her legs went weak. Her knees would have buckled if he hadn't caught her arms. "Chase. My God..."

"Easy. I've got you. You're okay."

She wasn't okay. She tried to tell him about the two men, but her throat closed up. Tears from the gas and smoke, and from relief, welled in her eyes.

"Hang on to me," he said.

The next thing she knew she was being swept off her feet and into his arms, solid as stone. She hung on for dear life as he took her up the stairwell at breakneck speed. She could feel his muscles bunching beneath her, could hear him grunting with the effort.

An instant later, he slammed his palm against a door and they entered a dimly lit hall. The air was clear, but Lily couldn't stop coughing. Her throat felt as if it were on fire. Gently, Chase lowered her to her feet, but her knees turned to mush.

"Easy." He steadied her. "Slow, shallow breaths. That's it."

Lily looked at him through gas-induced tears and struggled to get oxygen into lungs that seemed to be locked down tight.

Chase was breathing hard and coughing, too. A sheen of sweat coated his forehead and soaked his shirt beneath his arms and on his back.

"You got your feet under you?" he asked after a moment.

Lily wasn't yet sure, but she nodded.

"Good girl." He released her. "I'm sorry about the gas, but there was no other way."

"They were going to kill me. Kill the baby."

But he was already looking over his shoulder. "Honey, we've got to run. Can you do it?"

The hall seemed to tilt, then her balance leveled. Lily's knees wobbled, but held. As if reluctant to let her go, Chase glanced toward the door from which they'd emerged. "We've got to go," he said. "Those sons of bitches will be here any second."

"I can do it," she heard herself say.

He didn't look convinced. Snarling something beneath his breath, he darted to a fire emergency box, broke the glass and jammed the large hose nozzle between the door and the handle.

"That's not going to keep them out," she said.

"Might buy us a minute or two."

"Chase, damn it, there's nowhere to run."

"Let me worry about that." He took her hand and squeezed it hard. "I'm not going to let anyone hurt you. You got that?"

She nodded.

Giving her a half smile, he took her down the hall at a controlled sprint. Lily held her protruding abdomen with one hand and struggled to keep up. Behind her, she heard pounding on the door. Fear sent her pulse back into the red zone.

The hall turned and then widened. Beyond, against the dim light of a battery-powered light, Lily saw people milling about in the main hall. Chase led her toward a rear exit door. Without pausing, he hit the push bar with both hands and sent the door flying.

Daylight encompassed her; the air eased the burning in her throat. She had no idea what time it was, only knew she was grateful for the light.

They cut through throngs of people who'd gathered on the sidewalk. Several people protested as Chase shoved them out of the way, but no one tried to stop them.

They hit the sidewalk along Summer Street and headed east toward the Summer Street Bridge. More than anything, Lily wanted this terrible ordeal to end. She desperately needed to stop and rest. She needed to know what was happening and why. But she knew if she stopped now, the men would catch up with them.

The air turned humid and smelled of the harbor as they stepped onto the bridge over the Fort Point Channel. At the apex, Chase finally pulled her to a stop.

For several seconds the only sound came from their labored breathing and the hard thrum of her own heart.

"You okay?" Chase asked.

"That's a damn silly question at this point," Lily snapped.

He glanced down where she gripped her belly with her left hand and he grimaced.

"I can't run anymore," she said.

He reached out as if to touch her abdomen, but dropped his hand. Lily saw the strain in his face, the worry in his eyes. She knew him well enough to know that worry had nothing to do with him and everything to do with her and the baby.

She followed his gaze as he looked up and down the channel. Twenty yards away, a small boat chugged toward the bridge.

Chase glanced back toward South Station, and a chill ran down Lily's spine. "Do you think you can make it across the bridge?" he asked.

She nodded.

"I want you to go to the other side. There's a small pier there with a dock on the left side and a sidewalk in front of the office building. Go to the waterfront sidewalk and wait for me."

"We're splitting up?" She hated the alarm in her voice, but she was not equipped to handle this kind of situation alone.

"I'll be there. I promise. Go."

The sound of gunfire erupted from the general vicinity of South Station. Chase glanced that way, then turned back to Lily. "That's your cue, honey. I want you to run as fast as you can to the other side of the bridge. Can you do that?"

Without waiting for an answer, he stepped away from her and gave her a gentle shove in the direction he wanted her to go.

Shocked he would suggest they split up and frightened by the sound of gunfire, Lily turned back to him. "Where are you going?"

"I'm going to get us some transportation." Giving her a cavalier grin, he climbed onto the low rail at the edge of the bridge. "Run," he said. "I'll be there in two minutes. I promise."

At that, he looked down at the water and jumped into space.

LILY RAN as she had never run before. Gripping her belly with her right hand, she sprinted toward the far end of the bridge. In the distance, she could see the Boston Convention Center and, beyond, the giant cranes of the waterfront district where container ships were loaded and unloaded.

Her uniform shoes pounded the sidewalk like pistons. Above her labored breaths she heard shouts and a volley of gunshots from behind her. But Lily didn't slow down. There was no way she was going to let those men with guns get their hands on her again. She ran for her life.

Her heart felt as if it would explode in her chest by the time she reached the other side of the bridge. Following Chase's instructions, she veered right and took the crumbling steps to an old wooden pier. Exhausted, her back aching with renewed fervor, she dropped to her knees and gulped great lungfuls of air.

Vaguely, she was aware of the rumble of a boat's engine as it pulled up to the dock. It crossed her mind that the men had once again found her. Fear gave her the strength to raise her head. A quiver of uncertainty went through her when she saw a man tie off the boat and approach her.

A little voice inside her head warned her to run. But she was too damn tired and in too much pain to move. She didn't have much fight left in her. Heart pounding, she watched the man approach, realizing belatedly his form was familiar. One she would know anywhere, even in the dark of night.

"Hey, it's me."

Chase's voice washed over her with the comfort of warm waves lapping sun-washed sand. Setting his strong hands beneath her arms, he lifted her to her feet. "Easy. You're going to be okay. I've got you."

"Where did you get the boat?" she asked, getting her legs beneath her.

"Let's just say I borrowed it and leave it at that, shall we?"

But Lily knew that wasn't the case. He'd stolen it. He'd jumped from the bridge onto the boat's deck and commandeered it from some hapless boater. But she was too tired to argue with him about any of it. Chase might like living on the edge, but she knew him well enough to know that in the end he'd make things right.

"We've got to get out of here." Taking her arm, he started toward the boat.

For the first time, Lily got a good look at the vessel. It was a small Bertram Yacht about twenty-five feet long with an inboard engine and a flying bridge. The name painted on the fiberglass hull almost made her laugh.

The Sea Escape.

Chase helped her onto the boat and dashed to the helm. Reaching down, he flipped several switches then turned a key. The engine choked out a groan and rumbled to life.

Spinning the wheel, he glanced over his shoulder at her. "Get below deck."

Lily didn't argue. She tugged open the door to the main cabin. Her back spasmed as she went down the steep steps, and pain gripped her midsection hard enough to make her double over, but it passed quickly.

Below deck, the air was warm and smelled pleasantly of eucalyptus. A tiny kitchen lined the port side. Aft, a small cubbyhole-like bedroom replete with fluffy pillows and several nautical blankets beckoned.

Weak with exhaustion, back pain and

the aftereffects of adrenaline, Lily kicked off her uniform shoes and took the single step up to the sleeping quarters. Just for a little while, she assured herself and crawled onto the mattress.

Within minutes of closing her eyes, she drifted into darkness.

THE HAIRS ON CHASE'S NECK prickled uncomfortably as he steered the small Bertram Yacht between the piers beneath the Summer Street Bridge. From above he could hear the two gunmen arguing. He couldn't make out their words above the rumble of the engines and the wind that had kicked up off the ocean to the east, sending the dark clouds skidding across the sky, but he knew they were ticked off because their prey had gotten away.

Sweat trickled between his shoulder blades as he idled beneath the Congress Street Bridge, hopeful the jacket and hat he'd found on the boat shielded him from detection.

The water grew choppy as he steered the vessel beneath the Evelyn Moakley

Bridge. Normally, the high-rise buildings of Boston's financial district would be waking up shortly, the lights, computers and machines coming to life, the traffic snarled, the pedestrians harried. Today, the buildings would stand vacant. It was as if, despite the daylight, the entire world was still trapped in a never-ending blackout.

Keeping his eyes on the bridges and the sidewalks that ran across the channel at city-block-sized intervals, Chase took the Bertram past the John Joseph Moakley Courthouse and headed southeast toward the World Trade Center. More than anything, he wanted to find a safe place for Lily. A place where they could park the boat and he could make some calls and figure out what was going on.

Easier said than done with a blackout to contend with, armed gunmen shooting at them at every turn—and a very pregnant and exhausted woman in tow. But Chase admitted Lily Garrett was not just any pregnant woman. She was the woman he'd once loved more than his own life. The woman who carried his child. The only woman who'd ever gotten to him. The one woman capable of tying his gut into knots.

Spinning the wheel, he made a sharp left into a small marina where fishing boats, a popular Boston dinner cruise ship and a few sailboats bobbed in their slips. Flipping a switch on the control panel, he idled as quietly as possible into the marina.

All the slips were occupied, the boats tugging restlessly against their moorings. Chase was just about ready to give up on finding a slip when he spotted an empty one next to a good-size tug. Ever watchful for the harbormaster, Chase quickly parked the boat, cut the engine and then jumped onto the dock to tie the moorings to the cleats.

Once the boat was secured, he opened the hatch and stepped into the below deck cabin. He threw off the jacket and hat. There was no sign of Lily.

Worry trickled through Chase in the instant before he spotted the forward sleeping quarters. Heart skipping, he strode to the tiny room and ducked inside. Something warm and jumpy ran the length of him when he saw Lily. She lay on her side with a blanket pulled up to her shoulders.

In the dim light coming from the galley, he could just make out the lines of her body. The soft, pale glow of her face. Her dark eyes and full mouth. Her womanly curves. The round shape of her swollen belly. For several seconds he stood there, staring at her, uncomfortable with the emotions tearing through him. He knew he should turn away. Make some calls. Try to figure out what the hell was going on.

But his legs refused the command. He couldn't stop staring at her and thinking about all the intimacies they'd shared. He'd never experienced such passion before in his life. Standing there, he couldn't deny that he wanted to touch her again.

He'd never seen Lily as vulnerable. She was opinionated and vocal, one of the most capable women he'd ever known. But lying there, sleeping, carrying his child, she looked incredibly vulnerable.

Scraping a hand over his jaw, he turned away.

Her voice stopped him cold. "Chase?"

He didn't turn to face her. Gripped by emotions he hadn't felt for a very long time—emotions he didn't *want* to feel—he took a deep breath and told himself they would pass. Damn it, they would.

"What's going on?"

It was a question he couldn't ignore, even if he didn't know the answer. She deserved to know what was happening. At least he could tell her as much as he knew.

Slowly, he turned. She was sitting up with the blanket pressed to her breasts. Most of her hair had come loose from the ponytail and cascaded like curly red strips of silk around her shoulders. In the past, she'd always hated her hair, threatening to color or straighten it. Chase, on the other hand, had always loved it just the way it was, as soft and bright and fragrant as sunshine.

He studied her, loving the way she looked at this moment, and he wished he could capture this image of her and emblazon it onto his memory. "We're safe for now," he said in a thick voice.

"Who are those men and what do they want?"

"I don't know. I'm going to make some calls, see if I can get some answers." He started to turn away. "Go back to sleep."

But she was already scooting off the edge of the small bed. "Like I can sleep."

He knew it was silly, but he stepped back when she stood. He'd been close to Lily a hundred times in the months they'd been together. But he didn't want her close to him now. He wasn't sure what he'd do. Something stupid, more than likely.

"You were doing just fine a moment ago."

Because he didn't want to make a mistake he'd regret, he left the sleeping quarters and strode to the galley. Pulling the security guard's cell phone from his belt, he sat at the small table, punched in the number for Ben Parker and waited.

The FBI agent picked up on the first ring.

Chase didn't waste any time. "They found us at South Station."

"How did they know you were there?"

Something uncomfortable pinged in the

back of Chase's brain. How *had* the men known where to find them? Ben was the only person who'd known where they were.

"Good question," Chase said.

"You sweep yourself for transmitters?"

"I checked my clothes."

"Kind of haphazard, Chase."

"Yeah." He paused, troubled by the suspicions leaching into his brain. "I'll figure it out."

Ben continued. "Look, I got a call from Ethan—"

"He okay?"

"He's worried about you. Said you were talking and the line went dead."

"Sons of bitches ambushed me."

"You okay?"

"We're fine." Keenly aware that Lily was standing just a few feet away, listening, Chase lowered his voice. "These bastards have pulled out all the stops, Ben. They're gunning for us big time."

"You still going to come in?"

Chase hesitated, some obscure little voice warning him to trust no one. "Did you check with Fort Leavenworth?" The military prison administrators would have been able to tell Ben if Liam Shea had been released or escaped.

"He was released last summer."

"Damn." Liam Shea now took front and center on his list of suspects. He'd made an explicit threat. The modus operandi fit his style; he was an expert on anything electrical. Chase couldn't think of anyone else who might be holding a grudge and held the power to orchestrate these kinds of ambushes.

"Anyone else come to mind?" Ben asked.

"I think Liam Shea's our man." Chase considered the situation. "Is Vice President Grant still missing?"

"Last update I received from Quantico, he was. Some reporter got a hold of the story. Most of the radio stations are running on generated power. Now it's all over the news."

"Anyone claim responsibility?"

"Not yet." The other man paused. "The police lab put a rush on the blood found at Hancock Tower. It's been positively identified as the vice president's."

"You think he's still alive?"

"No way to tell." He sighed. "I sure as hell hope so. This is unprecedented."

"Any word from Shane?"

"I talked to him briefly. He was ambushed, but he's fine. I'm telling you, all hell has broken loose."

Remembering the cell phone he'd taken from the gunman, Chase said, "Can you run a number on a cell phone and see if anything pops up?"

"Whose?"

"I got it from one of the goons. Chances are it's a disposable and he didn't use his real name. But criminals can be incredibly stupid sometimes."

"Worth checking." Ben Parker fell silent while Chase gave him the number. Then he said, "I think you and Lily should try again to come in. Let us set you up in a safe house until this situation stabilizes."

"Not yet."

"Chase…at least bring *her* in. For God's sake, if she's pregnant and these bastards are trying to—"

"I'll keep her safe," Chase interjected,

not wanting to hear the way the other man was going to finish the sentence. "I'll keep both of them safe."

As he disconnected, he prayed to God he could keep his word.

Chapter Seven

"We lost them."

Aidan Shea paced the elegant confines of his hotel room, but he barely noticed the opulent furniture or the sumptuous food, crystal and silver spread out on the linen-draped table before him. Every ounce of his attention was focused on the two men delivering the exact news he didn't want to hear.

The men didn't look too worried about their failure, a fact that didn't elude Aidan. Over the years, more than one good man had made the mistake of thinking Aidan was nothing more than a computer geek and a loner.

If only they knew.

Damn them both. Damn Chase Vickers. And damn his nine lives straight to hell.

"Where did you lose them?" he asked, the softness of his voice belying the rage boiling just beneath the surface.

The man wearing the wing-tip shoes shifted his weight from one foot to the other. "The waterfront."

"Big place," Aidan said. "Lots of hidey-holes for the rats."

The other man brushed at a nonexistent speck of lint on his thousand-dollar suit jacket. "Vickers might be good at what he does, but he can't elude us forever."

Seeing an opening to inject good news, the other man came to attention. "He's got a pregnant woman in tow. They can't have gotten far."

Idiots, Aidan thought, and turned on him. "Don't make the mistake of underestimating Chase Vickers," he snapped. "As far as you know they could be out of the country by now."

The man in the expensive suit looked chagrined. "We've got every available man working to contain the area. We've got perimeters set up. It's only a matter of time before we smoke them out."

"Time is the one thing we don't have!" Aidan brought his fist down on the table hard enough to send a crystal tumbler over the edge.

"I'll make some calls—"

"Calls? How the hell is making a phone call going to solve this problem you've created?"

The other man stepped in to take some of the heat off his counterpart. "I thought—"

"Don't think!" Aidan shouted. "Act! I want them caught yesterday! You got that? I don't care what you do or how you do it! Find them."

"We'll find them." The man in the wing-tip shoes met his gaze and a silent understanding passed between the two men.

Within the pale blue depths of the other man's eyes, Aidan thought he saw a smidgen of grit, of cold determination, the icy fortitude of a killer, and he was marginally relieved. He and his brothers and father had paid top dollar to these brutal men. Men who didn't ask questions and got results no matter how distasteful the task. He hoped they hadn't wasted their money. Aidan was starting to think he'd be better off finishing this alone.

But it was too late. Boston was a huge city. He didn't want to be the one to tell his father Chase Vickers had gotten away.

"Find Lily Garrett," he said after a moment. "Bring her to me."

"What about Vickers?"

Aidan Shea smiled. From what he'd seen, big, bad Chase Vickers was like a puppy dog when it came to Lily Garrett. "Bring me the woman, and he will follow."

LILY FOUND cold ham, some smoked cheese and a bottle of grape juice in the galley. As Chase finished his call, she gathered plates and glasses and set them on the table. In one of the cupboards, she discovered a box of stale crackers. Normalcy in the midst of lunacy, she thought as she arranged crackers on the plate next to the cheese.

Chase looked at the table as if the concept of eating were foreign.

Lily motioned toward the food. "I know eating seems mundane in light of everything that's happened."

"No," Chase said quickly. "You need to eat. You're…" His words trailed.

She couldn't withhold the smile. "Eating for two."

Chase smiled back, but it looked tense on his face.

Taking the bench seat, Lily set a slice of cheese on a cracker and popped it into her mouth. Chase poured grape juice into glasses. For several minutes neither of them spoke; the only sound came from the gentle lapping of waves against the hull.

"You're really worried, aren't you?" Lily asked. It was a profound question, because Chase wasn't the kind of man to worry.

"Worry is an understatement."

"Do you have any idea who's behind it?"

"Maybe."

She arched a brow, wondering if he was going to keep her in the dark.

"There was a mission, eleven years ago," he began. "Things went wrong and some hostages were killed. A man was court-martialed and went to prison."

"And?"

"He was recently released."

"Who is it?"

He grimaced. "Look, I think the less you know the better off you'll be."

"So you're going to keep me in the dark?"

"I just think there are some things we shouldn't talk about," he said carefully.

"If something happens…" Not sure how to finish the sentence, Lily let her words trail. She didn't want to think about anything catastrophic happening. Not to her. Not to Chase. But she had her unborn child to think about now. She had no choice but to consider every possible scenario no matter how distasteful.

"If something happens," she began, "I need to know what to do. I need to know where to go. I need to know who to trust."

Rising abruptly, Chase crossed to the small stove and leaned. Lily held her ground, taking in the rigid set of his shoulders and white-knuckled fingers. She could practically feel the tension coming off him. All she could think was that this wasn't the Chase Vickers she'd once known. That man had been totally un-shakable. He'd thrived on danger, gotten off on adrenaline. What had changed?

"You think if they get their hands on me, they'll torture me for information about you?" she asked.

He gave her a dark look, the muscles in his jaws working. "That's where they'll start."

A powerful shudder ran the length of her, followed by a burst of cold, hard fear. Not so much for herself, but for her unborn child. How was she going to keep her baby safe when she couldn't even keep herself out of harm's way?

"I'm not going to let those bastards get anywhere near you." Grinding his teeth, he brought his fist down on the counter hard enough to rattle a saucepan. "Damn it."

"You're worried about the baby," she whispered.

He spun on her. "I'm worried about both of you!" As if realizing he'd shown her more emotion than he should have, he lowered his head and raked a hand through his hair.

She used to love running her fingers

through those light brown tresses, long and always unruly. Every time they made love she'd—

Chase's words cut off her reverie. "This shouldn't have happened. Damn it, Lily, you shouldn't be in this situation."

"I am. We can't change that. Now we have to deal with it."

He looked up at her and his gaze burned into hers with such intensity that she thought she could feel the heat emanating from its depths.

"The man I've been talking to is Ben Parker," he spit. "He's an FBI agent." He shook his head. "I just don't know who I can trust anymore."

"You don't trust Ben?" When he didn't answer, she said, "I see it in your eyes. I hear it in your voice."

He scraped a hand over his jaw. Lily couldn't ignore the scrape of whiskers against his palm. It was such an intimate, masculine sound. One she'd heard a hundred times before. One she'd always liked.

"I know this sounds crazy," he said. "Maybe even paranoid. But Ben knew we were at South Station and within minutes of my telling him, we were ambushed."

The words made her feel a little sick inside. As if they were up against something that could not be defeated. Setting her hand over her abdomen, Lily went back to the table and sat. "You think he revealed our whereabouts?"

"I don't know." He started to pace, restlessly eating up the width of the boat, like a tiger in a cage. "Ben is a good man. A good agent. He's tough, loyal as hell. Lily, you know I choose my friends carefully, and he's one of the best."

"Do you trust your instincts?"

"I used to." He laughed, but it was a dry, humorless sound. "Now I'm not so sure."

"What do we do now?"

"We stay put. Once I get you to a safe place, I'm going to figure out who's behind this. I'm going to stop them. Find their weak point. Keep them from getting to anyone else." Chase picked up the phone he'd set on the table, glanced at the display and laughed. "Phone battery is about shot."

"I saw some electrical components in one of the cabinets when I was looking for food. Maybe there's a charger we can use." Energized by the prospect of doing something proactive, Lily rose quickly. The stab of pain low in her belly came so hard and fast she couldn't withhold the gasp. Bending slightly, she grasped the back of the bench seat and leaned heavily.

"Lily!"

Before she could return to the bench, Chase darted to her and set his hand gently against the small of her back. With his free hand, he took her arm and guided her back toward the bench seat.

"What's wrong?" he asked. "Is it the baby? What?"

"It's okay," she said, more embarrassed than concerned. By the time she sat, the pain had already subsided.

"It's not okay. You're in pain. You practically doubled over. I saw your face."

"It happens every so often." Leaning back in the seat, she set her hand against her belly and smiled. "I think she's trying to tell me something."

Chase blinked. "She?"

She glanced up at him, more moved by his concern than she should have been. "It's a girl."

"A girl?" He gave her a look that made him seem just a little bit lost. "How do you know?"

"There's a test. A sonogram. If there's no…you know…then we know it's a little girl."

"Oh, okay." He gave her a lopsided grin. "Wow. A little girl."

Lily couldn't help it. Maybe it was the stress of the situation, or the lack of sleep, but she laughed. It was the first time she'd seen tough guy Chase Vickers speechless, and she couldn't help but indulge.

"What's so funny?"

"You."

The concern etched into his every feature softened. "I'm glad you find me so amusing." Surprising her, he smiled, and for several seconds they grinned at each other like a couple of fools.

The moment shifted when Chase lifted his hand and set it against her face. His palm was warm and slightly rough against her cheek. Lily had seen that look in his eyes before. She knew what would happen next. And while the intellectual side of her brain told her to pull away, a treacherous part of her brain refused to let her move.

"I love your smile," he said thickly. "I love it even more when you laugh."

"Nothing about this is even remotely funny." She'd hoped the words would snap them out of whatever stupor gripped them.

They didn't.

Stepping closer, Chase lifted his other hand, ran his fingertips across her cheek and through her hair. All the while he searched her face with an intensity that held her spellbound. "I've missed you," he said.

"Don't." Her word came out as little more than a puff of breath.

"Too late." Tilting his head slightly, he brushed his mouth across hers.

The initial shock of pleasure curled her toes. Her body tingled with sensations she'd forgotten existed. Lily was no stranger to intimacy. But only in this man's arms had she ever felt true passion. *Not now,* was all she could think, but he'd been right. It was too late to stop....

Need vibrated through her with such force that her knees went weak. Intellect warred with a sudden, jarring stab of desire that went from her brain to every erogenous zone in her body.

"Wait," she whispered.

Chase didn't wait. His hand slid from her hair, down her back where he gripped her and pulled her snug against him. His body was like a stone wall against hers, all sinew and muscle and tightly restrained male need. Lily wanted to believe that's all this was. Lust caused by months of celibacy. The aftereffects of adrenaline and fear. High danger and higher emotion.

But one look into his eyes and she knew this moment was so much more. And while the little voice of reason screamed for her to stop, her body moved closer. The ridge of his erection nudged her swollen belly and a pang moved through her. Locking his arms around her, he devoured her mouth. A powerful wave of desire swept the length of her when he used his tongue and went deep.

Lily didn't think. Her mind couldn't form so much as a single rational thought. But then it had always been that way between them. Chase induced a desire too powerful to contain. *Fool,* the little voice accused. But she banished it.

Vaguely, she was aware of his hands sweeping down her back, brushing the outsides of her breasts. A shiver barreled through her. She didn't intend to put her arms around him, but the next thing she knew her arms looped around his rock-hard shoulders that trembled with re-straint. She kissed him back with equal force, equal passion. Their tongues tangled, breaths mingled. All Lily could think was that she wanted more. If she didn't get it she would die right here in his arms.

Slowly, he backed her toward the small table. When the backs of her legs bumped into it, he lifted her and stepped between her knees. Desire like she'd never before known knifed her. She went wet. Forget-ting about all the reasons she shouldn't respond, Lily wrapped her arms around him and kissed him with a desperation she didn't know existed. She was keenly aware of his arousal against her. His labored breaths in her ear. Her own labored breathing rasping from her throat.

It was too much. It was too good. Too late. Too damn insane…

Turning her head, Lily broke the kiss. As if realizing for the first time what he'd done, Chase stepped quickly back. His shocked expression met hers. But within the depths of his topaz eyes, Lily saw all the other emotions he was usually so adept at hiding. She saw affection and shock and the undeniable realization that there was unfinished business between them.

"I didn't mean to do that," he said.

Unable to hold his gaze, Lily slid off the table. Wrapping her arms around herself, she walked to the other side of the galley and looked out the tiny nautical window. She didn't know what to say. She didn't know what to feel. The only thing she knew for certain was that as long as she lived, there would be no other man who could ever make her feel the way Chase Vickers did.

That fact frightened her almost as much as the men with guns.

CHASE COULDN'T BELIEVE he'd kissed her. Couldn't believe he'd crossed a line he'd sworn he wouldn't. He chided himself as he stood on deck. Of all the stupid and impulsive things he could have done, getting physically close to Lily was the most self-destructive.

He'd always prided himself on his ability to keep his emotions and his physical needs in check, especially when it came to his job. But then came Lily Garrett with her sunny smile and kind heart, and his resolve had gone right down the tube. She was his one and only weakness. She was a weakness so powerful it scared the hell out of him. When it came to wanting her, every logical thought, every hope of self-preservation, went by the wayside.

Even after she'd sent him packing, he had pined for her. It was a pathetic image to say the least. But Chase had ached with missing her, with wanting her back in his life, and not just for a little while. No, Chase Vickers never did anything halfway. He'd spent months in a black hole so deep he thought he'd never find his way out. His job with Eclipse was the only thing that had saved him. Then, of course, he'd taken it to the extreme, taking on every suicidal mission offered.

Hell of a way to heal a broken heart.

Broken heart?

Where did *that* come from? Chase wanted to deny that Lily had the power to hurt him. No woman did. He'd seen to it. With every relationship, he'd made certain he never crossed that line. Once he realized things were getting too hot to handle, Chase walked away and never let himself look back.

Lily was different. He hadn't been able to walk away no matter how hard he'd tried. She'd gotten under his skin, into his head, into his heart. Twenty minutes ago, when he'd taken her into his arms and kissed her until they were both breathless and dizzy and half-insane with wanting more, Chase would have sold his soul to the devil to get her back.

"It's only lust, you idiot," he muttered into the darkness.

But the words rang false.

Now Lily was pregnant with his child. He'd brought danger to her life and into the life of their unborn child. It was the one thing she'd always made clear she wanted no part of. She hated his secret work. She hated the danger, the uncertainty, the unpredictability. Early on, he'd laughed at her fears. He'd assured her he was too careful and too damn good at what he did for anything to happen. Not only to him, but anyone he got close to. After all, he took the utmost care to keep his personal life far removed from his professional life.

Evidently, he hadn't been careful enough.

Lily had been right. Her worst fears had become reality. The irony of that burned like a red-hot branding iron.

Around him, even though it was barely dawn, the waterfront was alive with activity. It seemed as if the city hadn't slept at all during the long dark hours of the blackout. Chase had to figure out what to do next, how to keep Lily safe. He had to get out of this mess alive and find the person responsible.

Pulling the cell phone from his belt, he snapped it open. He was in the process of punching in Ty's number yet again when he glanced down at the display. His heart sank when he found it dark. Just like everything else in this godforsaken city. Not to mention his own mood.

Angry and frustrated, he headed toward the hatch to search the cabinets for a possible charger. He needed communication. He needed to find out if Ty and Ethan had been ambushed. More than anything, he wanted to get to the bottom of what was going on and track down the son of a bitch responsible.

He descended into the galley, hoping Lily was asleep. He didn't want to face those pretty green eyes. Eyes that accused him of everything he'd always denied. More than anything, he didn't want to face his own shortcomings. The fact that he'd been wrong. His attraction to her. And the terrible mess he'd made of their lives.

Fate didn't see fit to grant his wish. He

found her sitting at the small galley table, gripping a steaming cup as if it were her last lifeline to the world. She watched him descend the steps with the wariness of a hunted animal, as if he posed as much danger to her as the men hunting them.

"I thought you'd be sleeping," he said.

"I tried." She shrugged. "Can't."

"Too wound up, probably." He frowned at the cup she held. "Are you sure you should be drinking coffee?"

"It's tea." She smiled. "I think caffeine is the least of my problems."

Pulling a mug from the cabinet, Chase took a moment to gather his thoughts, an impossible task considering how jumbled his emotions were. When he turned to face Lily, she was still watching him. Still wary. So beautiful and fragile, he wanted to reach out and touch her just to make sure she was real.

"I'm sorry about…earlier," he said.

She looked away. "Things are pretty confusing right now."

"It's easy to get caught up in things. In the past."

She motioned toward the stove. "Water is still hot if you want some tea."

He didn't, but he poured it anyway so he'd have something to do with his hands. He hated feeling so awkward, hated the way she looked at him as if he were a danger to her. He hated even more the hard reality that he wanted what he could never have.

"So what do we do now?" she asked.

When he ran out of things to do at the stove, he carried his cup to the small window and looked out. "I need to recharge this phone." But the charger he found in the cabinet Lily directed him to didn't fit. Disgusted, he finally sat at the table across from Lily.

For a moment, the only sound came from the gentle lap of water against the hull. "How long is this blackout going to last?"

Chase shook his head. "Ben Parker told me two power plants were taken out."

"My God. Sabotage? Why would someone do that?"

"I think maybe it's all related. The synchronized ambushes. The kidnapping of the vice president. The blackout."

She set down the cup. "Is this about you? About your…work?"

"I think so."

"But how is the vice president involved?"

He sipped the tea, but he didn't taste it. Taking a deep breath, he told her more about that mission-gone-bad from over a decade ago, and Liam Shea's role in it.

"They're not going to stop, are they?" she asked.

"Someone is going to have to stop them."

"You?"

Chase didn't answer. At the moment, unarmed and left without communication and transportation, he was in no position to stop anyone.

"We can't hide out here forever," she said. "You know sooner or later they'll find us. Is there some place safe where we can go?"

"I've been racking my brain, trying to come up with a place."

"A safe house?"

He shook his head. "There's only one place I can think of, but it's out of the city. I'm not sure we can get there."

"Because of the traffic jams?"

"The streets and highways are jammed with cars. Tow companies are working, but many of them are inoperable because very few have access to gasoline, thanks to the blackout. I had a hell of a time getting to the Hancock Tower. I imagine all the major highways are jammed. People were panicked, thinking this blackout was some type of terrorist act. Thousands of cars ran out of gas where they sat in traffic. Everything's blocked."

"What place do you have in mind?"

Ugly thoughts entered his mind, and Chase hesitated. No one knew about his half-brother's house in New Hampshire. It was a virtual fortress.

But while his half brother's compound offered safety for Lily, it was the last place Chase would ever want to go himself. While he and Shane worked well together on their Eclipse missions, it had been years since they'd had a brotherly relationship. Chase resented his half brother. Shane reminded him of a time in his life he'd rather forget. A time when he was ten years old, alone for the first time, and powerless to change any of it. He'd worshipped his older brother. But Shane hadn't cared. Hadn't even noticed. And when their mother had died, Shane had gone off to college and Chase had been relegated to foster care where he traveled from family to family until he was eighteen and joined the military.

Was he willing to set the injuries of his past aside? To keep Lily safe, he was. Chase turned to her. "Shane's," he finally replied. "My half brother. He lives in New Hampshire. He's a security expert. The best, in fact. His house is the only secure place I can think of."

"How do you know these gunmen haven't gone after him, too?"

"They have. But I can tell you it didn't happen at his house. If we can get out of town, I can stash you there. Make some calls, try to figure out what the hell is going down."

She stared at the cup of tea that had long since gone cold. "This baby means everything to me. I can't let anything happen to her."

"I'm not going to let anyone hurt either of you."

She raised her eyes to his. "You can't guarantee that. No one can."

He leaned close. "I said I'm not going to let anything happen to you. I mean that."

Her gaze searched his. After a moment, she pursed her lips. "So, do you think we can make it to your brother's house?"

"We have to try." He glanced toward the window. "Sooner or later they're going to find us. We have no communication, no means of transportation. Limited ammo. Our best bet is to run."

Tightening her mouth as if in determination, she nodded. "Let's do it."

"You sure you're up to it?"

"I'm not going to sit around and wait for them to ambush us again." Rising, she crossed to him, her eyes direct and burning bright. "But let me tell you something, Chase. Once we're safe, I want you to go. I want you out of our lives for good. I can't let you or your lifestyle place this baby in danger again."

Chase thought he'd been prepared; he'd

known that when this was over they'd go their separate ways. But hearing the words aloud cut with a brutality he hadn't expected. The pain that followed sucked his breath right out of his lungs.

The instant he'd realized she was pregnant, that the baby was his, he'd resolved to provide for them financially. Monthly support. A college fund for the baby. Maybe a house. It was the very least he could do. After all, he'd been paid handsomely for the work he'd done for Eclipse. He lived simply, had few needs. The money he'd socked away would more than take care of the baby. And Lily, if she'd let him.

He didn't allow the next thought to materialize. The one where some treacherous little voice told him he wanted more. That he wanted to know his child, to be part of his child's life. Part of Lily's life. He wasn't going to go there. Damn it, he wasn't.

Chase shoved the thoughts away, jammed them into the deep dark hole where the rest of his emotions lay stagnant. He didn't need them. He didn't need anyone.

Picking up his cup, he took it to the sink and dumped it forcefully. He could feel Lily's eyes on his back, but he didn't turn to face her. He didn't want her to see the pain and anger he knew were in his eyes.

He was about to escape above deck when movement from outside the tiny nautical window caught his attention.

"What is it?" Lily whispered.

"They found us," Chase said, and slid the revolver from his waistband.

Chapter Eight

Footsteps from above deck made the hairs on Lily's neck prickle. Someone was on board the boat. At least two of them; she could hear them talking in low voices.

She swallowed a gasp when the doorknob to the cabin rattled.

"Damn thing's locked," said a male voice with a strong Bostonian accent.

"Kick it in like you did the other one," said another voice. "Boss told us to find them, so we gotta search all the boats, not just the easy ones."

"You sure this is the boat?"

"How do I know? Kick the damn thing in."

The next thing Lily knew she was being pulled backward by Chase's strong hands.

A crash sounded in the general vicinity of the door. Then she was in the fore sleeping quarters. Next to her, Chase worked frantically to unhinge and open the deck hatch, his eyes never leaving the thin door he'd latched behind them.

The hatch sprang open. Chase looked at her. "I'm going through, then I'll pull you through. Once we're on deck, I want you to run. Don't wait for me. Don't look back. You got that?"

She looked at the small hatch, her stomach plummeting. "I can't fit through there."

He looked at the hatch, looked at her bulging abdomen. His mouth opened, but for a moment nothing came out. "Okay. Plan B." He looked around wildly. "Hide. In a cabinet. Under a blanket. Whatever. I'm going to go up, circle around and ambush them."

Unable to speak over the rapid-fire beat of her heart, Lily nodded her head.

Chase looked as if he wanted to say more, but another crash sounded from the cabin. The boat rocked slightly, and Lily knew the men were coming down the stairs and into the galley to search for them. If the men opened the door, they would find them both.

Giving her a final look, Chase heaved himself through the hatch. Panicked, she looked around for a place to hide. Several compartments lined the walls, but none of them were large enough for her to get inside. Realizing she had no alternative but to get under the blanket and pray it bought her a few precious seconds, she lay down and pulled it over her head.

The knob to the sleeping quarters rattled. "It's locked, too," said the man with the Boston accent.

"Kick it down. I'm going to the next boat."

The door burst open. She heard heavy breathing, the rustle of clothing, a whispered curse. Minutes stretched like hours as he began checking compartments. In the next instant, the blanket that covered her was jerked roughly away. Gasping, Lily sat up and found herself facing a dark-haired man with large features and the deadly blue steel of a pistol.

"I'll be damned," he said. "Must be my lucky day."

Lily caught a glimpse of a dark blur coming at her from behind the man. An instant later the man grunted and pitched violently forward. In the light slanting through the port window, she recognized Chase as the attacker. Relief mingled with shock at the sight of him in action. His lips were peeled back in a snarl, his eyes as dark as night.

The other man tried to defend himself, but he was no match for Chase. Several well-placed punches and the man crumpled.

Chase's attention flicked to her. "You okay?"

"I am now." She looked past him toward the cabin door. "What about the other guy?"

"Out cold."

She glanced down at her would-be attacker. "Who is he?"

"I don't recognize him." Frowning, he bent and quickly rifled the man's pockets. "No wallet. No ID."

"By design?"

"More than likely." Chase smacked the man lightly on the cheek several times to rouse him. "Wake up, jackass," he snapped. But the man didn't stir.

Cursing, Chase grabbed him beneath the shoulders and dragged him up the steps onto the deck. "Start the engine," he said over his shoulder to Lily.

Her legs shook as she climbed the steps. In the darkness, she saw Chase lift the unconscious man, cross to the gunwale and dump him unceremoniously onto the wooden dock. Turning, she searched the instrument panel for a key to start the engine, but her hands shook violently.

She jumped when two strong hands came down on her shoulders.

"Easy," Chase said from behind her. "It's just me."

"I can't find the key," she blurted.

"I've got it." Moving to her side, he tilted his head as if to get a better look at her, his expression intensifying. "You're shaking like a leaf."

"I'm scared," she admitted. "That was really close."

"I know." He turned her toward him, made eye contact. "We're going to be okay."

At the moment, Lily didn't think anything would ever be okay again.

"Why don't you go below deck and get some rest?" He punctuated the words by looking over his shoulder. "We have to get out of here. Judging from the way things are going, there are more where those two came from."

She followed his gaze, incredulity rising inside her at the thought of some faceless, nameless person sending more gunmen. "When will this nightmare end?"

He twisted the key and the engines rumbled to life. "When I end it."

Lily watched him traverse the impossibly narrow side deck to the fore deck where he slid a knife from his belt and slashed the moorings. He looked her way as the boat came free. "Get that last rope, will you?" he shouted.

Glad for something to do, Lily headed toward the aft deck. As she reached for the rope attached to the cleat, she spotted two men twenty yards away on the dock, walking toward them. "Chase!" she whispered. "Over there!"

The next thing she knew, Chase was beside her. He brought the knife down on the rope, severing it with a single slash. "Get below deck." Not waiting for a response, he took her arm and ushered her toward the cabin door.

Lily swung open the door but didn't go inside. There was no way she could hide out below deck and leave Chase to face this alone. At the very least she could keep watch. It would be only a matter of seconds before they were spotted.

A few feet away, Chase darted toward the bridge, where he slid behind the instrument panel. She could see the men walking the dock, eyeing each boat they passed. She knew the moment the taller man spotted them. He stopped dead in his tracks and pointed.

"They've seen us!" she said to Chase.

"Hang on." The engines revved as he backed the boat from the slip. He glanced over his shoulder where the men had broken into a run toward them, then jammed the throttle forward.

Lily grasped the safety rail next to the

control console just as Chase gunned the engine. The Bertram shot away from the slip like a racehorse out of the gate. Water spewed high into the air. Chase hit the trim with the heel of his hand and the vessel smoothed out.

A gunshot sounded over the roar of the engines. Lily glanced toward the newcomers, saw them stop at the edge of the dock, weapons raised. The boat was thirty feet out and moving rapidly away from the dock, but there was no way it could outrun a bullet.

One of the men fired off two shots in rapid succession, one of which ricocheted off the outrigger inches from her head. Clinging to the safety rail, Lily watched him line up for another shot while the other man spoke into his cell phone and gestured wildly.

Chase took the boat toward the channel, but Lily knew it was only a matter of time before the men came after them.

In moments the dock faded away. Just as she turned to go below deck, the unmistakable sound of an engine sounded behind them. Already, the men had found a boat.

"My God, they're coming after us!" she shouted to Chase.

He glanced over his shoulder and cursed.

"How did they get a boat so quickly?" she asked.

"Same way we did," he said. "Stole it."

A high-pitched zing zipped past her ear.

"Get down!" Chase shouted.

Thwack! Thwack! Thwack!

A volley of bullets slammed into the starboard side of the cabin and the window. Plexiglas and fiberglass exploded, raining down shards on her. The boat lurched. Lily glanced up to see Chase cut the wheel hard to the right. She lost her balance, made a wild grab for the bridge ladder but missed. Terror arced through her like lightning as she reeled backward toward the gunwale. All she could think was that she was about to be flung overboard.

"Lily!"

Chase's voice cut through the jumble of fear. A scream tore from her throat as she lunged toward the bridge ladder and grabbed the bottom rung with her right hand.

"I'm okay," she called out.

"Hang tight!" he shouted. "Don't move!"

Lily hung on for dear life as he swung the boat left in an effort to avoid another volley of bullets. Unable to make it below deck, she clung to the ladder and prayed they survived the ride.

CHASE TOOK the Bertram out of the marina and into the seaport channel, its hull slicing through the water at a dangerous speed. Channel traffic was heavy for this early-morning hour. It seemed more than one boater had taken to the water to ride out the massive power outage, where they had all the comforts of home thanks to engines and batteries.

Chase made the turn and entered the main harbor, but only a fraction of his attention was on outrunning the bastards behind them. He couldn't get the image of Lily clinging to the ladder out of his head. She'd come very close to going into the water. She'd come even closer to getting shot. The thought of her being hurt, or worse, filled him with a cold, hard terror he'd never before experienced, even in all the years he'd been with the military and Eclipse.

He didn't like what that told him about his frame of mind. The bottom line was he was letting his emotions get in the way. A mistake he'd seen many a good man make—and pay dearly for in the end, either with his own life, or someone else's.

Chase wanted to blame his lack of clarity on fatigue or adrenaline or maybe even his lack of communication and tools. He wanted to blame it on anything but the truth: his feelings for Lily and the child she carried.

He tried not to think of that as he shoved the dual throttles forward as far as they would go and headed north. He could see Logan Airport to his right, the Water Transportation Terminal to his left. Twenty yards behind him, a fast-approaching vessel told him they weren't making much headway.

He pushed the Bertram as hard as he dared, until the odometer needled well into the red zone. But the yacht was no match for the smaller vessel zigzagging through the water twenty yards away.

"They're following us!"

He glanced to his left to see Lily standing at the bridge ladder, clinging to a rung. More than anything, he wanted to stop and make sure she was all right. He wanted to touch her, take her into his arms and promise her that he would keep her safe.

There was no time for any of that.

Chase used every nautical skill he'd ever acquired to outrun the speedboat. He thought he heard gunshots, but the sounds were drowned out by the roar of the wind and the scream of the engine. A dozen boats appeared ahead, stopped and bobbing in the choppy water. Red and blue strobes flashed, and he realized they'd encountered some kind of police blockade. He could hear a voice booming over a loudspeaker, but he couldn't make out the words. Did the blockade have something to do with the kidnapping of the vice president?

Chase made a sharp turn toward the New England Aquarium. Beyond, he could see the low profile of the Long Wharf Marriott Hotel and Christopher Columbus Park. Knowing they weren't going to be able to escape on the water, Chase headed toward the park.

If he and Lily could disembark safely and he could get his hands on a car, they would be home free. No one could outdrive Chase Vickers. He could lose them in the chaos and traffic then drive Lily to Shane's house in New Hampshire. From there they could put their heads together and try to figure out what the hell was going on.

Chase didn't slow when he entered the hotel marina's no-wake zone. Twenty yards from the dock, he cut the engines and cranked the wheel hard to the right. The Bertram slipped sideways through the water. Chase saw the pier approach at an alarming rate of speed. Old tires were chained to the concrete piers as bumpers. Hopefully, the rubber padding provided by the tires would be enough to keep the impact from breeching the hull.

"We're going too fast!" Lily shouted behind him.

"Hold on!"

Chase jumped from the bridge to the

deck. Lily spun toward him, terror registering in her eyes. A glance at the dock told him they would impact in just a few seconds. Wrapping his arms around her, he pushed her to the deck just as the big boat slammed into the pier.

Fiberglass crunched as the pier tore into the starboard hull. The impact knocked him hard against the live-bait well, but he rolled and was able to use his body to protect Lily.

Abruptly, the vessel went still. Chase jumped to his feet and looked around. His legs were shaking. He glanced down, saw Lily on her hands and knees, and guilt stabbed him like a dagger.

"Easy does it." Bending, he set his hands on her shoulders and gently helped her to her feet. "Are you all right?"

Brushing flyaway hair from her eyes, she raised her eyes to his and jerked her head once. "That was some parking job, Vickers."

"Miscalculated. Came in too fast. Guess I'm getting too old for this."

An emotion flashed in her eyes, but it was gone so fast he wasn't sure of its meaning. He glanced over his shoulder at the mouth of the marina. He saw the men in the speedboat fifty yards out. He could hear the engine idling down.

"Let's get out of here." Stepping onto the gunwale, he took her hand and helped her onto the dock. "We need a car."

"Do you know someone in the area?"

He shook his head. "Might have to borrow one."

"What's one more felony on top of a dozen others?" Glancing back at the damaged Bertram, she choked out a laugh. "Remind me not to ever let you borrow my car."

"Spoilsport." Spotting the low profile of a well-known waterfront hotel, he took her hand. "Come on. There's a parking garage not far from here."

They left the dock and crossed the asphalt to the grassy plain of Christopher Columbus Park. Chase felt exposed being out in the open. Every couple of seconds he looked over his shoulder.

Hand in hand, they crossed Atlantic Avenue. Chase was keenly aware of Lily's hand, small and warm within his. Midway down the block, he spied a six-level parking garage.

"This looks like a good place," he said.

"What about the security guard?" Lily pointed to a windowed booth where a lone attendant read a book.

"That's why they make back doors."

"I was afraid you were going to say that."

Chase was familiar with the garage; he'd parked here once or twice before, when he'd had business downtown. It was always packed with vehicles. The key was going to be finding one that was unlocked. People were so damn security conscious these days.

They crossed a quiet side street to an exit where a row of three mechanical arms stood in the down position. Ducking under the farthest arm, Chase led Lily to the rear of the garage where he went from car to car, checking each for an unlocked door.

He tried six cars before finding one that wasn't locked. The four-door Toyota sedan wasn't his vehicle of choice; he much preferred good old-fashioned American engineering and a gas-guzzling, muscle-car engine, but it would do in a pinch.

"No keys," Lily pointed out. "How do we start it?"

He couldn't help it; the way she'd used the word "we" made him grin. Standing there in her scrubs and swollen belly, she did *not* look like a car thief. "That's the easy part." He opened the passenger door for her. "Hop in and belt up."

Lily settled herself into the passenger seat. Giving the parking garage a final sweep, he opened the driver's side door and went to work on the ignition wiring beneath the steering column. "I never liked these foreign electronics."

"Makes stealing a car so inconvenient," she muttered.

Just then, the starter kicked and the engine turned over. "Ah, that's my girl." Chase slid onto the seat, strapped in and put the car in gear. "Next stop, Shane's."

Chase didn't want to go there. He didn't want to be indebted to his half brother. After what Shane had done to him eighteen years ago, Chase didn't care if he ever saw him again. But he would have to put the old hurts of a ten-year-old boy aside. With Lily's life at stake, neither of them had a choice.

"It's out of the city," he said. "You'll be safe there. And it will give me the chance to get to the bottom of this."

"Must be our lucky day." Lily had reached into the console. Smiling, she pulled out a cell phone that was plugged into the cigarette lighter charging.

"Looks like I picked the right car, after all."

The words were barely out of his mouth when he noticed the glint of headlights ahead. A car coming up the ramp at a fast clip. Too fast to be just another parking-garage patron.

"I think we've got trouble."

"Is it them?"

"That would be my guess."

The roar of an engine filled the garage. Tires screeched against the concrete floor as the car sped around the corner. It would be upon them in seconds.

"Here they come." Chase rammed the car into gear.

Lily stared at the shifter in horror. "Why can't we just duck?"

"If we don't get out of here now, we never will. Hold on." Praying he could get past the jammed streets, he floored the accelerator.

Chapter Nine

Lily was no fan of speed. She much preferred slow and steady and the assurance that she would get to her destination in one piece. Chase, on the other hand, didn't seem to know anything but one speed when it came to any vehicle equipped with an engine: fast. For the first time since she'd known him, they were in full agreement.

The Toyota jumped out of the parking space so fast she was thrown against her seat back. Headlights came at them from the right. Chase spun the wheel left. Tires screeched as the Toyota slid sideways. The next thing she knew they were zipping along the up ramp at freeway speed.

A glance over her shoulder told her the

driver behind them was no slouch when it came to speed, either. The car seemed to appear out of nowhere, gaining on them at an astounding rate.

"They're catching us!" she cried, torn between wanting to get away and wanting to slow down.

"Not for long."

At the top of the ramp Chase jerked the wheel hard to the right. The vehicle fishtailed, its left rear quarter panel slamming into the concrete barrier wall. The instant the tires grabbed purchase, he gunned the engine and they flew up to the next level.

"What are we going to do when we reach the top?" she asked.

"We go down and pray there's not another car in the way."

That left a little too much in the hands of Lady Luck for Lily's taste, but she didn't have time to voice her concerns. Chase took the car up another level, around another turn, tires screeching, engine revving so fast she thought it would blow.

By the time they reached the top, the

car pursuing them had fallen behind, but only marginally. Chase kept his eyes on the rearview mirror and drove like a madman. An instant before they began their descent, he reached into the waistband of his jeans and pulled out a pistol.

"Take this," he snapped.

"You're kidding."

"Put your hand out the window and fire off a few shots."

Lily stared at him, incredulous. "I've never fired a gun before in my life." But she took the gun.

Chase already had her window lowered. "We just want to slow them down."

The weapon felt cold and deadly in her hand. Lily turned in her seat. Chase made a sharp right turn, throwing her against the safety belt.

"Do it," he said. "Now."

Lily was right-handed, but she couldn't get a good angle, so she turned in her seat and put the weapon in her left hand. No time to aim. No time to think about repercussions. She pulled the trigger. The retort and the kick startled her so much she nearly dropped the weapon. But she didn't. Gripping it with a hand wet with sweat, she fired off two more shots. Chase accelerated down the ramp, his eyes flicking from the rearview mirror to the garage ahead.

The vehicle behind them spun left and then right, coming to an abrupt stop crossways on the ramp.

"Got 'em," Chase said.

Even though the men pursuing them meant them harm, the thought of shooting another human being made Lily feel sick. As if realizing the route her mind had taken, Chase glanced her way. "You shot the engine block," he said.

"Are you sure?"

"I saw the smoke. You did good."

Unable to hold the gun any longer, Lily dropped it onto the floor at her feet. She felt nauseated. Felt like crying. Simultaneously, anger coursed through her. Because anger was safer than falling apart, she held on to it for dear life.

Chase's voice curtailed her thoughts.

"Lean forward," he said. "Put your head

down, lace your hands over the back of your head."

A few yards ahead, Lily caught a glimpse of the mechanical arm. No time to argue. No time to debate the wisdom of crashing through the arm at breakneck speed. Thinking only of the baby, she leaned forward and braced.

An instant later, the car crashed through the arm. Chunks of wood flew in all directions. The vehicle bucked wildly as it flew down the final ramp. The tires barked against asphalt as the car went over a dip and then screeched onto the street. Chase cut the wheel hard to the right. Lily looked up, certain they were about to go into a spin. But Chase fought the wheel and managed to maintain control.

They hit traffic at Atlantic Avenue, but Chase took the Toyota over the curb and onto the sidewalk, laying on the horn to get two unwitting pedestrians out of the way. He crashed through a closed newspaper kiosk to get around a stalled delivery truck. Canvas and paper and fragments of wood billowed past the passenger window. Lily held on for dear life as he jumped the curb a second time and took them back onto the street.

They didn't speak until they reached the Charlestown Bridge on the north side of town. Stranded cars and delivery trucks were parked along the roadway like discarded Tonka toys, but the bridge was open. Chase took the loop to Interstate 93 and headed north toward New Hampshire.

"Should be clear sailing from here," he said.

Lily didn't know whether to laugh or cry. If she laughed she would surely become hysterical; if she cried she might not be able to stop. She wasn't sure which would be worse. So much had happened in the past few hours. Her life had changed drastically. Not only because she'd faced death, but because a man she'd thought was out of her life forever was back, and her heart was telling her nothing had changed.

Too many emotions jammed her heart, overwhelmed her mind. All the old feelings were still there, like a dormant fever, waiting to erupt. He was a good man. He'd saved her life multiple times tonight. But he'd also been one to bring danger into her world. Most troubling of all was the knowledge that he'd introduced that same danger into her baby's life, too.

How could she have such powerful feelings for a man who would undoubtedly bring worry and pain and possibly future danger into her life?

Lily didn't know what to do. She didn't know what to feel. Emotions coiled and churned inside her like a cauldron of acid eating her alive. As they sped past the state line into New Hampshire, the dam finally broke. Leaning forward, she put her face in her hands and began to cry. Not just a little, but great shaking sobs she felt all the way to her belly. She wasn't sure why she was crying; tears never helped anything. But exhaustion and fear and adrenaline had a way of breaking a girl down. Combine that with her conflicting feelings for Chase and she had an emotional meltdown on her hands.

"Lily."

Chase's voice carried over her sobs,

broke into her thoughts. But she couldn't answer. Didn't want to look at him. He was an astute man, and she wasn't exactly sure what her expression would tell him.

"Honey, what's wrong? Are you in pain? Is it the baby?"

Taking a deep breath in an effort to regain control of herself, she risked a look at him. If she hadn't been crying, she might have laughed. Of all the harrowing experiences they'd weathered, he looked most frightened at this moment.

"The baby's fine."

"What is it, then?"

Not sure how to answer, Lily wiped her eyes and turned to the window. A breath shuddered out of her and the sobs subsided. But she couldn't stop thinking about how close they'd come to getting killed. That because of Chase, a man she cared for deeply, she had come very close to dying before giving birth to their innocent child.

The thought broke her heart—and drove home the fact that she could not let herself get entangled with him again.

"Hey," he said gently, "what is it?"

She jolted when he reached across the seat and covered her hand with his. "I can't talk about this right now," she said.

"Talk about what?"

"I don't want to talk to you."

That silenced him; she could practically feel his mind spinning through possible reasons for her behavior. But he didn't release her hand. "Honey, if you're hurting, you need to tell me."

The statement almost made her laugh. Physically, she was fine. For the most part, anyway, considering the stress of the past hours. Emotionally, she was, indeed, hurting. She was frazzled and more confused than she'd ever been. Before this day, she'd known beyond a shadow of a doubt where she was going and who she was. She'd formulated a life plan for herself and her unborn child. Then Chase Vickers had waltzed back into her life and thrown her neat and orderly plan into total disarray.

"Lily, talk to me."

She didn't even look at him. Instead, she stared through the window at the eastern sky where the sun peeked through the dark clouds. A new day, she thought, and promised herself she would not repeat the mistakes of her past.

THE SLAMMING OF A CAR DOOR jolted Lily awake. She wasn't sure how long she'd been sleeping, but it was fully light. The car was parked in a neat gravel lot surrounded by lush maple and sycamore trees. A manicured lawn stretched to a tiny Victorian-style cottage nestled within another copse of trees.

She glanced over to see Chase slide behind the wheel. Though he'd been up the entire night, he looked rested, relaxed and...breathtakingly handsome.

Not wanting to go there, she sat up and looked around. "What time is it?"

"Almost eight."

"Where are we?"

"Midway to Shane's house. I haven't been able to reach him on his cell, so I thought we'd stop and get some rest, eat and shower up."

The thought of a shower appealed to her

immensely. Even more appealing was the thought of food. Having not eaten a meal since before her shift at the hospital, she was famished. And exhausted. Aside from a couple of catnaps, it had been almost twenty-four hours since she'd had any real rest. As Chase crossed in front of the car and opened her door, Lily didn't miss the fact that he scanned the quiet, tree-shrouded road, and she wondered if either of them would be able to relax long enough to sleep.

He offered his hand, but Lily didn't take it and struggled from the passenger seat on her own. He pretended not to notice the slight. Thunder rumbled in the distance as they stepped onto the small wooden porch of the cottage Chase had rented from the manager of the cottage colony about a quarter mile up the road. Lily glanced over her shoulder to see dark clouds billowing and she knew before long they would get rain.

Chase used the key and swung open the door. Lily smiled at the sight of the charming room. It was small but tastefully decorated with dark antique furniture. Two full-size beds were covered with cream and navy matching comforters. On the center night table, a fake Tiffany lamp cast a circle of warm yellow light. A print of a Monet seascape hung on the wall above a tiny round table.

The room smelled pleasantly of sandalwood and lemon oil. Lily walked past the beds and spotted a dozen votive candles on the vanity. None of them were lit, but she could smell the vanilla from where she stood. Under the right circumstances, she might have enjoyed staying here. But the circumstances were anything but ideal. *Except for the man*, a traitorous voice interjected.

"I thought I'd run out and get us some food."

Lily turned to find Chase standing just a foot away, watching her. She acknowledged the worry in his eyes, and promised herself she wouldn't let his concern for her get to her no matter how handsome he was. No matter how powerful her attraction to him.

"I'm starving," she managed after a moment.

"I wish I could offer you more than a burger and fries."

"Believe me, a burger and fries will not be a hardship."

He shifted his weight from one foot to the other. "Do you need anything else? Toiletries? There's a drugstore in town."

"A strawberry shake."

A smile emerged and it changed his entire face. His topaz eyes shimmered like some tropical sea on a sunny day. Laugh lines appeared on either side of his chiseled mouth. Lily found herself thinking of the kiss they'd shared back in Boston and an emotion she did not want to acknowledge stirred deep inside her.

"I'd forgotten about your weakness for ice cream," he said.

Returning the smile, she pressed her hand to her abdomen. "You know. Hormones."

He glanced toward her belly. For a moment, Lily thought he was going to cross the distance between them, perhaps set his own hand against the place where she carried his child. She held her breath, not sure what she would do if he did so. Would she step back? Or would she share the moment with him? Or maybe step into his arms the way she had seven-and-a-half months ago...

The sound of car tires crunching over gravel made her jump. A cold finger of fear skittered up her spine when Chase went to the window, parted the drapes and peered out. When he turned to her, his face was solemn. "Just a family pulling into another cottage down the road."

"You sure?"

"Yeah." He offered a dry smile. "Screaming kids. There's no hit man alive who would brave that in the name of cover."

The humor was lost on Lily. Her imagination had already gone into overdrive. "What if those men followed us? What if they find—"

"No one followed us," he interjected. "I promise." He glanced toward the door. "Look, I'm going to go pick up the food. Why don't you lie down and relax for a while."

Lily didn't want to admit she was frightened to stay here alone. She'd always prided herself on her independence. But the past several hours had proved to her she was light-years out of her element. This was the one time when she welcomed his protection.

As if reading her thoughts, he stepped forward and set his hand against her cheek. "You'll be fine for a few minutes," he said gently. "I promise. I'll be right back." He grinned. "Think strawberry shake."

Lily managed to smile back. "I'm going to hold you to it."

"Wouldn't have it any other way," he said, and slipped out the door.

After watching him pull away, Lily didn't waste any time and headed directly for the bathroom where an antique clawfoot tub beckoned. She turned on the faucets and stripped. On the vanity, she found a sample-size bottle of scented bath crystals, shampoo and a fancy little soap made in Paris. The small, everyday items seemed ridiculously luxurious in light of the past hours, and she took full advantage.

After lighting the candles, she found a fluffy white robe hanging at the back of the door and draped it over the towel rack near the tub. Steam rose from the water as she stuck her toes into the bubbles to test the temperature. Sighing with pleasure, she stepped into the tub and sank into bubbles until they tickled the bottom of her chin.

Outside, rain had begun to fall. She could hear fat drops pinging on the roof and window. Distant thunder rumbled. Inside, the scents of lavender and vanilla floated lazily in the air. Slowly, the warm water lulled her into the state of relaxation she sought.

She tried not to think about Chase. There was no way she could sort through all of her conflicting feelings for him. Just because he was the father of her child didn't mean she would fall for him again. It didn't mean they were going to have any kind of relationship. Lily had made that decision months ago and she intended to stick with it.

But when she closed her eyes, it was Chase she saw, his topaz eyes looking at her as if she were the only woman in the world. His hands, smooth as silk, running through her hair, skimming down her body. His hard mouth finding hers, trailing kisses to places that caused her to shiver with delight…

"Cut it out," she murmured. "He is *so* wrong for you."

Wiping the unwanted and totally inappropriate thoughts of him from her mind, she leaned back and closed her eyes. Just for a few minutes, she promised herself, and let herself drift.

PARKED AT THE REAR of Beefy's Burger Palace, Chase pulled the cell phone from his pocket, thankful for some battery life, and quickly dialed Ben Parker.

The other man picked up on the first ring. "Where are you?"

"New Hampshire." Chase got right to the point. "Any news on Shea?"

"We've got every available agent on it. It's been tough because of the blackout. We're looking hard, but so far we have nada."

Chase muttered a curse. "I need to talk

to Ty and Ethan Matalon. I haven't been able to reach them on their cells. I also need Shane, but he's not picking up." Static sounded and he tapped the cell phone. "My damn phone is about to die."

"I'll keep trying them for you and have them contact you." A thoughtful pause ensued. "Are you and Lily all right?"

"For now. I lost them, but these bastards are relentless."

Ben paused. "Did you know Liam Shea has three sons?"

"Now that you mention it, I do remember hearing that in the years I worked with him." Something pinged in the back of Chase's brain. "You think the sons picked up where their old man left off?"

"Loyalty can be a powerful motivator."

"Especially if they think their father was somehow wronged."

"I'll get on the horn. See what else I can dig up on them." Ben Parker fell silent for a moment. "Look, the offer still stands if you want me to get you set up in a safe house."

"I'm taking her to Shane Peters's house."

"Your half brother? I thought you two were on the outs?"

"We are, but I know he'll come through on this."

"Where's his house?"

Chase hesitated, not wanting to get too specific. He'd always trusted Ben. But if the FBI agent was playing both sides of the coin, Chase needed to know. Setting a trap was the only way to smoke him out. He'd already decided to tuck Lily away in a motel before arriving at Shane's house, in case he walked into an ambush. If he did, he would know Ben was a spy. "It's about fifty miles from here. Near the town of Bretton Woods. Can you give Shane a call and let him know to expect me? Let him know we're going to need some additional security."

"You got it."

The phone beeped. Chase looked down, saw that the battery was just about dead. "I gotta go, Ben. I'll try to pick up another phone or get this one charged."

But the line was already dead.

"Damn it."

Looking in both directions, Chase

pulled onto the rain-slicked street and headed toward the cottage. The aromas of burgers and French fries filled the car, making his mouth water. When he looked over and saw the strawberry shake, he thought of Lily and smiled.

What the hell was he going to do about her? About the baby? About his feelings for them? Chase had decided a long time ago he couldn't be with her. Not on a long-term basis, anyway. Not that she would have him, he reminded himself. Chances were, she wouldn't want him in their child's life, either.

Could he live with that?

The truth of the matter was Chase wanted to know his child. He wanted it so much his chest ached with it. But how could he when Lily was so adamant about not wanting him around? Even if she agreed to some sort of visitation, how could he be around her and not go mad with wanting her? There was no way he could settle for just being friends with Lily. He would always want more. If he got the chance, he would *take* more. But he knew it would invariably cost him a piece of his soul.

To make the situation even more complicated, after the past hours, he had to take into consideration the possibility that his presence might place them in danger. It was a terrible dilemma to which there was no easy resolution.

The harsh realities of the situation he faced ate at him like acid as he parked outside the cottage and killed the engine. Gathering the food and drinks, he left the car, unlocked the cottage door and entered. The first thing that struck him was the silence. He'd expected to open the door to find Lily sitting on the bed, sleeping or watching television.

Where the hell was she?

Alarmed, Chase set the bag and drinks on the small table. Pulling the pistol from his waistband, he crept into the room and silently closed the door behind him. He checked the closet, found it empty. He could hear the hard thud of his heart, feel the edgy snap of adrenaline. Fear pulsed through him in a terrible rush.

With the stealth of a predator, he sidled to the bathroom. Using the muzzle of the gun, he eased open the door. Only then did he notice the swirling steam, the scents of lavender and vanilla. A few feet away, Lily lay back in the claw-foot tub, a wet cloth over her face.

The sight of her froze him in place. For a moment, he could do nothing but stare. She'd piled her hair on top of her head in an unruly mass. Red tendrils curled around her face. Her throat was long and elegant and impossibly delicate. Lower, he could see the tops of her breasts where a tiny heart pendant lay against porcelain flesh. He'd given that pendant to her two years ago. He'd forgotten about it until now, and he wondered why she still wore it.

Fragrant bubbles concealed the rest of her, but Chase had seen every beautiful curve before. Every lovely detail had been branded onto his brain. The soft fullness of her breasts, the deep hue of her nipples, the silky softness of her flesh. His hands had caressed every inch of her and his mouth had explored every delicate spot. He remembered the way she sighed when he pleasured her, the way she'd cried out his name when he brought her to peak—

"What are you doing?"

Lily's voice jerked him from his improper reverie. Feeling like a lecher, Chase quickly averted his eyes. "I just…" His words trailed when his eyes were once again drawn to her. His brain told him to look away, but his eyes refused.

Grabbing a towel from the rack, Lily covered herself as she stood, then wrapped it around her. Bubbles slid down wet flesh. The scents of vanilla and lavender swirled inside his head, drugging him like some powerful narcotic.

"You just what?" she snapped. "Is something wrong?" Never taking her eyes from his, she stepped from the tub. Holding the towel to her breast she jerked her clothes from the vanity. "Chase, you're frightening me."

Realizing she'd misunderstood his transfixion, he put up his hands. "I'm sorry. We're safe. It's just that I saw you and…" Not knowing how to finish the sentence without admitting something he did not want to admit, he turned away and left the bathroom.

He stood in the center of the room for several minutes and tried to get his breath back. He couldn't believe she could render him speechless, unable to move or think. Him. Chase Vickers. A man who could drive a speedboat at over a hundred miles per hour and not even get his heart rate up. He could consort with some of the most ruthless killers in the world during under-cover operations and not even break a sweat. But one look at Lily Garrett lying in a tub full of bubbles, and he felt as if he were aeons out of his league.

"Chase."

He didn't turn at the sound of her voice. He didn't think he could bear to see her in that towel again and not do something stupid. Like pull her into his arms and kiss her until neither of them could think straight. Or maybe tumble her into bed and ease some of the sexual tension that had been zinging between them since the start.

Only then did he realize that bringing her here had been a mistake. A big mistake that in the long run would probably cost both of them more than they bargained for.

"You okay?"

He actually jolted at the sound of her voice. He jolted again when she touched his arm. Her fingertips felt cool and soft against his suddenly feverish skin. Chase knew the signs. Racing heart, sweating palms, the rush of blood to his groin. It wasn't the first time lust had gripped him when it came to this woman and it probably wasn't the last. The problem was, his feelings for Lily went a hell of a lot deeper than simple male lust, and he couldn't do a damn thing about it without digging a hole so deep he might not ever find his way out.

"I'm fine." Moving away from her, he crossed to the table and stared down at the food he'd brought. He tried to conjure his hunger from earlier. But food wasn't what he wanted. It wasn't what he *craved*, what he needed more than his next breath.

"Any sign of the men?" she asked.

"No."

"Any news on what might be happening?"

Knowing he couldn't put off the inevitable, he finally turned to her and immediately wished he hadn't. The oversize terry-cloth robe wrapped around her made her look incredibly small and feminine. Her hair was still piled messily on top of her head. Wet tendrils curled around her face and stuck to her throat. Her green eyes were so clear and lovely he thought if he got any closer to her he might just fall into them.

"I talked to Ben Parker before the battery died." His voice grated like a coffee mill, so he cleared his throat. "He's going to let Shane know we're on our way. He'll be expecting us."

"What about Ty and Ethan?"

"Couldn't call them." He tapped the cell phone clipped to his belt.

Turning, she started for the phone on the night table. "You could call them from here."

She picked up the phone to hand it to him, but Chase was instantly at her side. Taking her wrist, he usurped the phone and recradled it. "Not on this phone. If Ty's or Ethan's numbers are bugged, the call could be traced back to this room."

"I didn't think we'd be here that long." She glanced down to where his large fingers were wrapped around her wrist, then slowly raised her gaze to his.

Chase knew he should let her go. He should turn around, walk over to that table, unwrap his food and forget about the crazy thoughts jumping through his brain. He didn't let her go.

She stared up at him, her expression startled, like a little cat snared in the jaws of a pit bull. "What are you doing?"

"Making a mistake, probably."

"Then be smart about this and stop it before it happens." But she made no move to pull away.

"We both know I've never been smart when it comes to you."

"We've gone down this road before," she said. "It didn't work the first time, and it won't work now."

"You sure about that?"

"I'm sure that mistakes are never a good thing."

She made a halfhearted attempt to loosen his grip. He didn't oblige. This wasn't easy for him. He wasn't going to make it easy for her. There was something between them. Heat. But something deeper. A connection so powerful he could feel it all the way to his bones. He was going to make her acknowledge it. He was going to make her remember.

"That's where you're wrong," he whispered. "This one is going to be good."

Taking her face between his hands, he lowered his mouth to hers.

Chapter Ten

Lily resisted the kiss. She resisted the physical pull to him. The emotional pull. But kissing Chase Vickers was like stepping onto a raft and barreling down a white-water rapid toward a waterfall. All Lily could do was hang on for the ride and hope she survived the fall.

Two seconds into the kiss and her heart began to knock hard against her ribs. Pleasure pounded through her, fighting with the warning blaring inside her head for her to stop before the situation spiraled out of control. But deep inside she knew that had already happened. None of this had been in her control since the moment she'd laid eyes on him back at the hospital.

His mouth moved over hers, stealing her breath and the last remnants of her rational thought. She pushed at his shoulders and made a sound of protest. But her efforts were halfhearted at best, a token effort she was bound by her own self-respect to make, and they both knew it. But then it had always been that way between them. Passionate. Skating the edge of control where there was no room for logic or right or wrong or smart.

"God, I've missed you." He trailed kisses down her throat. "I've never stopped wanting you all this time. Staying away from you nearly killed me."

"Nothing's changed," she said breathlessly. "You're still traipsing off to godforsaken countries and getting shot at. You're still keeping secrets about your work."

He looked at her. Lily saw heat and desperation and what might have been regret in the depths of his eyes. She felt all of those same emotions in her own heart.

"None of that changes the way I feel about you," he said. "It doesn't change what's between us."

"There can't be anything between us anymore."

"You can say that all you want. But you don't believe it. I know you feel what I do. I see it in your eyes. I feel it in your body when I touch you."

The image of him touching her came to her unbidden. That night he'd come to her apartment, the night she'd conceived the child she carried now. His hands had scorched her flesh. His mouth had devoured hers. His body had moved within hers as they'd made passionate love. It had been the most erotic experience of her life, the memory of which sent a powerful shiver through her.

"When I touch you here..." His hand brushed the sensitized tip of her breast. "You feel it here." He set his other hand over her heart, and his eyes burned into hers. "Your heart is racing."

It was true. Her pulse beat like a jack-hammer. She could feel her heart pumping superheated blood to every cell in her body. Her swollen breasts ached to be touched. Seven-and-a-half months pregnant, she'd never imagined she could feel the kind of desire cutting through her at this moment. Leave it to Chase to prove her wrong.

Lily's vision blurred when he tilted his head and kissed her neck. His whiskers chafed her flesh, sending gooseflesh down her body. Wanting more, she threw her head back and gave him full access. His lips burned her skin, hot and wet. His tongue swept over her, making her want him with a madness she'd never known.

A gasp escaped her when he took her nipple into his mouth. The pleasure knifed downward all the way to her womb, powerful enough to make her groan. She shivered when he parted the robe and cool air washed over her breasts, her swollen belly.

"You're beautiful." He set his hand over her belly. As his eyes met hers, she saw within their depths a reverence she'd never before seen. A mix of emotions that told her the man holding her cherished her, and he knew this moment was precious and fleeting and might never come again.

Lily smiled. "I look like I swallowed a basketball."

Chase chuckled and kissed the tip of her nose. "You're sexy as hell for a pregnant woman."

He made her feel beautiful, even when she wasn't. He made her feel like the only woman in the world. He made her feel precious and cherished. If only he would change...

"Chase," she whispered, "this can't go anywhere."

"That doesn't keep me from wanting you."

The truth of the matter was she wanted him, too. She wanted him with an intensity she'd never before experienced. Need ripped through her with every beat of her heart, with every breath rasping in and out of her lungs. And when she looked into his eyes, Lily was lost.

He lowered his mouth to hers and the kiss tore away the last of her resistance. His hands trembled as he loosened the belt of her robe and worked it from her shoulders. She shivered when the robe fell to the floor, but it wasn't from the cold.

Needing to feel the warmth of his flesh, she fumbled with his shirt buttons. Her fingers trembled, but he waited patiently while she undid them, one by one. Then her hands were on his chest where his own heart raged. Her palms brushed over his flat nipples and he shuddered.

"I need you," he said softly, backing her toward the bed. "I need you more than I need my next breath of air."

She wanted to believe he meant it on a physical level. Physical attraction was simple. But there was nothing simple about Chase Vickers. He was complex; he could be difficult. Rarely did he compromise. And she knew the meaning of his words went deeper than the flesh, edged into territory she'd spent the past seven-and-a-half months protecting.

She wanted to believe all the emotions rampaging through her were the result of physical attraction, as well, but Lily knew better. Even though nothing could ever come of her relationship with Chase, there was a small part of her that still loved him.

Her thoughts exploded into chaos when he eased her onto the bed and came down on top of her. Suddenly, her body was no longer hers, but that of a woman desperate for a man's touch. A woman who'd been alone too long. A woman who needed the physical love of the man who held her heart in his palm.

Chase kissed her hard, his mouth moving over hers with an urgency that fed the fire within her. But he was excruciatingly gentle with her body. He was careful not to put his weight on her belly.

He fumbled with the zipper of his slacks, then kicked them off. Sitting up, he pulled the comforter over them, then lay beside her so that they were nose to nose. "Can you...can you..."

She'd rarely seen Chase Vickers without words. Seeing him that way now charmed her. "Can I have sex?" she finished for him.

"Well...yeah. I mean, with the baby."

Lily couldn't help it; even though she was troubled by the high level of emotion between them, she smiled. "Somehow women have been managing that for thousands of years."

"Well, I've never done this with a pregnant woman before," he confessed.

"Me, either."

For a moment the music of their laughter filled the room. Lily laughed until tears squeezed from between her lashes. Then Chase put his hands on either side of her face. When she opened her eyes, he kissed her. The gentleness of the kiss devastated her. Longing that was both emotional and physical gripped her body, her mind, her heart.

"I love you," he whispered. "I always have, and I always will."

"I wish it was that simple," she said.

"It is. If you let it be."

"I can't."

"I know, honey." Looking deeply into her eyes, he kissed her again. "I know."

Desire spread through her like wildfire. She gave herself over to his kiss.

Pulling back slightly, he gave her a small smile. "I know this isn't going to solve anything. It's not going to fix the problem. But I want you to know you and that baby mean the world to me." He ran his palm over her cheek. "I promise I will never hurt you." He set his other hand over her belly. "I promise I'll never bring harm to our child."

Emotion gripped Lily with such power that she couldn't speak. She stared into his eyes while her heart beat out of control, and wished with all her might that things could be different.

He entered her with devastating slowness. Lily cried out with pleasure when he started to move within her. She'd been celibate since that final night with Chase. Since becoming pregnant, she hadn't seen herself as a sexual being. Once again, he proved her wrong. The sensations coursing through her body were more powerful than anything she'd ever experienced in her life. She could already feel herself barreling toward release.

As his mouth fused to hers and his hands caressed her, his body moved within hers until they became one. One body. One heart. One soul.

Completion crashed over her, a storm drowning a parched land. The power of it shook her, emotionally and physically. She cried out his name. Once. Twice.

He captured his name with a kiss. Shuddering with the power of his own completion, he wrapped his arms around her and whispered her name.

IT WASN'T OFTEN that Chase hated himself. He was generally well-adjusted; he was forgiving of his mistakes, and for the most part believed his good traits outweighed the bad. Today, staring at the ceiling with Lily warm and soft beside him, Chase loathed himself with a passion he could not describe.

He'd done the exact thing he'd sworn he wouldn't. He'd rekindled a fire that should have been left to die. A fire that was now burning out of control and threatening everything he cared for, everything he believed in.

Lily had been right all along; their relationship was destined for disaster. Regardless of his feelings for her, he'd had no right to get close to her or involve her in his life. He'd been a naive fool to think he could touch her and then walk away. But that wasn't the worst part of what he'd done.

He'd brought danger to Lily.

Cold terror swept up his spine at the thought of what he'd let happen. How could he have been so stupid? So utterly selfish? Why hadn't he listened to his intellect instead of his sex drive?

But Chase knew why, and the truth of it shattered every illusion he'd ever had about himself.

I love you. I always have, and I always will.

His own words rang like a death knell in his ears. For seven-and-a-half months he'd denied the truth. During that time, he'd been able to set his feelings aside by throwing himself into his work. He'd spent his days flirting with death. He'd tempted fate in so many ways he shouldn't even be alive. But no matter how hard he'd tried, there was one demon he couldn't exorcise.

His love for Lily.

At that moment Chase accepted the reality

that while he could banish her from his life, he would love her until the day he died.

Troubled by the thoughts running wild through his mind, he rose from the bed and strode to the window. Parting the curtain, he peered out. Storm clouds obscured the sun, and the sky hung low, much like his mood. In the parking lot, nothing moved. There were no cars. No men with guns. No sign of anything amiss.

God in heaven, what was he going to do about Lily?

There was only one answer. The one solution he did not want to face. The truth he'd denied because of his own selfish needs. Once this was over, he was going to have to let her go. He would stick around long enough to get her settled, to set up an account for his child.

And then he was going to have to walk away once and for all.

The thought of never seeing her again, never seeing his child, hurt. It hurt more than he could ever have imagined. But for the first time Chase was seeing the big picture. Contact with either of them would sooner or later place them in danger or get them both killed.

Decision made, Chase yanked his slacks off the back of the chair and stepped into them. When he was fully dressed, he sat on the bed and gently touched Lily on the shoulder.

"Hey," he said. "Wake up."

Stretching, she turned over, and the smile that followed devastated him. She was so lovely it hurt to look at her. He couldn't believe such a beautiful woman would have him.

"Hey," she returned. "What time is it?"

"Time to go."

She sat up and looked around. "How long did I sleep?"

"A couple of hours."

"Were you able to get some sleep?"

"Yeah," he lied.

She cocked her head, her eyes narrowing. "Are you all right?"

She'd always been perceptive when it came to his mood. His feelings were the one thing he wasn't good at talking about. As far as Chase was concerned, a man's emotions were a private thing. But Lily deserved to know what he was going to do and why. He needed to tell her the truth.

"We need to talk," he said.

"The men? Are they—"

"About us." His voice came more harshly than he intended. He'd never been good at delicate conversation. He only hoped he could do this without screwing up the situation more than it already was. "About what's going to happen when this is over."

Wariness entered her expression. "What are you talking about?"

"Being with you, like this, made me realize you were right all along." He shrugged. "I was wrong."

"Wrong?" She sat up straighter. "In what way?"

"Once this is over, and you and the baby are safe, I'm going to give you what you want, Lily, what you've wanted all along. I'm going to walk away." The words poured from him in a flurry now. "I'll find some way to get money to you. Take care of you financially. But under no circumstances can I ever see you again. And I can never, ever, see my child."

AFTER EVERYTHING they'd shared just a few short hours earlier, this was the last thing Lily had expected him to say. She told herself he was right. She told herself this was exactly what she wanted. After all, she'd done everything in her power to get this man out of her head, out of her heart. She'd almost convinced herself she'd succeeded.

But the instant he'd walked back into her life, all of the old emotions had bubbled to the surface. Lily had tried to deny them; she'd fought them valiantly. But her efforts had been in vain. The truth of the matter was, she loved him.

She would always love him.

How could she let him walk away when she'd finally faced the truth? But the bigger question remained. How could she let him into her life when his presence could very well put her child in danger?

The answer devastated her.

"Once I get you to Shane's place,"

Chase continued, "the FBI will pick you up. They'll debrief you. Put you up in a hotel temporarily, until we get this settled."

It was all happening too fast. Lily stared at him, not liking any of what he'd said. "I don't want to go to a hotel. I want to go home."

"If you want to keep your child safe, you don't have a choice."

It was the one point he could make that would convince her, and he knew it. While she couldn't dispute that he was right, she didn't like being manipulated. She didn't like being backed into a corner with no alternative.

"Chase, damn it, I want my life back. My job. My apartment. My friends." *I want you,* a traitorous voice added, but Lily dared not vocalize it.

"I know. I want those things for you, too. God knows you deserve them." He smiled, but it was brittle and maybe a little sad. "This is one of those times when we don't get what we want."

"What if they catch the men responsible?"

"Then you get your old life back." He

shrugged. "Things go back to the way they were."

That was what Lily had told herself she wanted throughout the entire ordeal. All she wanted was her old life back: her job at the hospital; her comfortable little apartment; a life where everything was neat and orderly and safe.

Then why did she feel as if her heart were being forcibly ripped from her body?

"What about you?" she asked after a moment.

He gave her a halfhearted smile. "I go back to doing what I do best."

"And what is that?"

"Keeping the bad guys away." One side of his mouth lifted into a smile that didn't come close to reaching his eyes. "Driving the limo."

Lily wanted to tell him that wasn't necessarily what he might be best at, but she didn't. Sad as it was, neither of them would ever know what kind of husband and father he would be. The thought broke her heart.

"All right," Chase interjected into her

thoughts, "let's pack up and get out of here."

As Lily stepped into her clothes, she told herself things were better this way. It was the clean break she'd been looking for all along.

But the rationalization didn't explain why she felt as if the world as she knew it had just come to an end.

Chapter Eleven

Chase made the call while Lily dressed in the bathroom. The cell phone was dead, but since they were about to leave, he took a chance and dialed Ben Parker's number from the cottage's phone. He needed to know if Ben had been in contact with Shane or if he'd gotten any information on Liam Shea's sons.

Ben answered on the first ring.

"This isn't a secure line," Chase announced without preamble. "What did you find on Shea?"

"We're still digging," Ben replied, "but so far we know that after the court-martial his wife, Margaret, divorced him and changed her name to Sullivan, her maiden name. Two of his sons, Colin and Aidan, moved to Washington State after their father went to prison. The third son is Finn. We don't know where he lives yet."

Chase wished for a laptop so Ben could send him photos. He had, after all, gotten a good look at the man who'd ambushed him back at Hancock Tower. In his gut he knew it was one of Liam's sons. If he could match the face to a photo, they might get the confirmation they were looking for.

Ben continued. "I pulled up federal records, and it looks like his sons kept in very close contact with Liam the entire time he was in prison. Lots of visits."

"Where's Liam now?"

"We sent an agent out there, but... Chase, he's nowhere to be found. Neither are the sons."

"I'll bet the farm they're behind this, Ben. Probably taking orders from their father."

"How do you know that?"

Chase reminded him of the foiled hostage rescue mission a decade earlier. "Liam was dishonorably discharged and court-martialed for disobeying a direct order. But he swore he was innocent. He swore one of the other men involved in the rescue mission framed him."

"Who?"

"I don't know. But Shea vowed revenge and he was dead serious about it."

"That kind of hatred would explain the lengths he went to in planning simultaneous ambushes. Maybe he's even responsible for the blackout."

"And Davis's kidnapping. He was involved in the failed rescue mission, too."

"I wasn't privy to all the details. That gives me more to work with. Now that I have more information to go on, let me do some more digging and see what I can come up with." Ben paused. "Are you still heading to Shane's?"

"Lily and I are en route now."

"Be careful, man."

Chase disconnected to find Lily standing just a few feet away, watching him. "Who was that?" she asked.

"Ben Parker. He's checking into my theory that Liam Shea is behind this."

"Can Ben arrest him?"

Chase approached her but stopped with two feet to spare. He didn't want to get too close. For the first time in his life, he didn't trust his judgment or his willpower.

Images of every intimacy they'd shared flashed in his mind's eye. Lily lying beneath him, her head thrown back in ecstasy, her hair spread out on the pillow like yards of red silk. He could still remember the way she breathed. The way she'd tasted. The heady scent of her skin filling his senses. The way her flesh had molded beneath his hands.

The urge to touch her was powerful, but Chase resisted. He couldn't risk making another mistake and drawing this out. One time was going to have to be enough.

"The less you're involved in this, the better off you'll be," he said.

"I'm already involved. I don't like being left in the dark."

Chase studied her face, soaking in her beauty, her kindness, the goodness in her heart. "We have to go."

She reached out and grasped his arm before he could turn away. "Don't lock me out of this."

Angry with her for pressing him when he'd asked her not to, angry with himself for bringing such ugliness into her life, he shook off her touch. "No."

Hurt flashed across her features, but he steeled himself against it. The last thing he wanted to do was hurt her. But life was full of pain, and there wasn't a damn thing he could do about it. At the moment he needed distance. Pushing her away was the only way he knew how to get it. For now his number one priority was to get her to a safe place. Once he did that, he'd walk away and never look back.

LILY STARED through the passenger window, watching the rain slide down the glass. Rolling farmland, miles of white rail fencing and the occasional farmhouse zipped by, but she barely noticed the pretty countryside. She couldn't stop thinking about Chase and the magic they'd shared.

And about the cold glint in his eyes back at the cottage.

They hadn't spoken since they'd climbed into the car and headed north on

Route 93 toward Shane's house fifteen minutes earlier. She told herself she didn't need him. Going it alone had been the plan all along. She was independent with a nice apartment and a career she loved. Not to mention a baby on the way. But deep inside, Lily acknowledged that she was lying to herself. No matter how much she wanted to believe it, her life would never be complete without Chase.

The terrible truth was that she still loved him. If she wanted to be perfectly honest with herself, she'd never stopped loving him. But Lily didn't want to be honest. Not when it was so much easier, so much less painful, to lie.

Damn him for doing this to her.

Damn her for letting him.

Leaning against the seat back, she shifted and tried to get comfortable, but couldn't. Her lower back ached. Her hips ached. She tried reclining her seat back so she could stretch out a bit, but it didn't help.

After several minutes of her fidgeting, Chase looked over, concern darkening his eyes. "Are you all right?"

"I just want this to be over," she snapped.

He glanced away from his driving to study her, but she looked away. She couldn't look at him without remembering what it was like to be held in his arms. She couldn't remember without wanting it to happen again. The reality that after today she would never see him again hurt more than she ever could have imagined.

She reminded herself that she had no future with Chase. She and her child would be safer and happier without him. But while her brain was telling her all the things she needed to hear, her heart begged to differ.

All the while, the pain in her lower back nagged at her with increasing fervor, setting her nerves on edge.

"We've got company." Chase's focus went to the rearview mirror, and he made a sound of disbelief. "They're not slowing down." He hit the gas. "Hang on!"

Lily was in the process of turning to look out the rear window when a crash sounded and the car jolted violently. At first she thought they'd hit something or had a blowout. Then she caught a glimpse of a vehicle behind them and realized they'd been rammed. "They're trying to run us off the road!"

"Or kill us," he said tightly.

The car jolted again and went into a skid. Gripping the seat, Lily glanced over at Chase. He fought the wheel for control.

"How did they find us?" she asked.

"I don't know." Chase cursed and shook his head. "I don't want to believe it, but Ben Parker was the only person who knew where we were."

"I thought he was—"

"So did I," he interjected.

Lily turned in the seat to see the chrome bumper and grill of a large SUV loom closer. "They're right behind us!"

The vehicle struck them again, hard enough to send the Toyota into a skid. Chase struggled with the wheel, but the car seemed to have a mind of its own. It crossed the yellow line, but within seconds he brought the vehicle back under control.

"Can we call someone for help? The police?" she shouted.

He didn't look away from his driving. "Battery's dead."

Like us, she thought and shuddered.

Another wave of horror ripped through her when the big SUV pulled up beside them. Lily caught a glimpse of the bumper and a shiny red fender. The silhouette of a driver and passenger behind tinted windows. An instant later, the vehicle swerved and crashed into them on the rear driver's side.

"Hold on!"

The vehicles clashed like two giant beasts locked in battle. Steel screeched against steel, mechanical screams that grated like fingernails on chalk. The Toyota shuddered and swerved, but Chase managed to maintain control.

"Can you outrun them?" Lily cried.

"Not in this thing. Whatever they've got is souped up."

She glanced over, saw sweat slick and shiny on his forehead. "What do we do?"

The SUV gave him no time to answer. The big vehicle slammed into them again. This time Chase was ready. He jerked the wheel hard, used the weight of the Toyota to hold his ground. The SUV backed off, falling in place behind them. But Lily knew it wouldn't last.

Turning in her seat, she saw the truck's bumper loom as the vehicle sped up and rammed them from behind. Lily tried to shout a warning, but she was too late. The Toyota fishtailed. Rubber barked against asphalt. Chase cut the wheel, but the vehicle went into a skid.

"Hang on!" he shouted.

The car spun sickeningly. Lily saw trees and a white fence flash by. Gravel and tufts of grass spewed high into the air as the car slid sideways over the highway shoulder into a ditch. A cry tore from her lips when the seat belt jerked painfully against her belly. Leaning forward, she put her hands over her belly in an effort to protect her child.

Finally the vehicle came to a stop. The next thing Lily knew, Chase was outside the car, yanking the door open.

"Are you all right?" he asked, unfastening her seat belt.

"I think so." She tried to get out, but a

cramp shot through her belly like a hot dagger. Choking back a groan, Lily closed her eyes and fell back against the seat. "Oh, God."

"Is it the baby,?"

"I'm hoping it's just a Braxton Hicks."

He looked blankly at her, but she knew there was no time to explain. He scanned the surrounding area for the SUV, but it was nowhere in sight.

"We're sitting ducks here." He yanked the pistol from his waistband. Somewhere in the distance, Lily heard an engine rev. And she knew the men in the SUV were not yet finished with them.

Chase knelt, his hand going to hers. "I need you to get out, honey. Right now, because they're coming back. Can you do that?"

The cramp had passed for the most part, but Lily felt another one waiting at the gate. Still, she nodded her head in acquiescence. Pain edged from her back to her abdomen as she slid from the car and straightened.

"Good girl." He guided her to the other

side of the drainage ditch toward a copse of trees. "This way."

She ground her teeth and put one foot in front of the other. "Where are we going?"

He stopped and motioned. "See that big red barn over there? I want you to run to it as fast as you can. Don't look back. Just run. Can you do that?"

Lily nodded, but she didn't know how fast she could run when the cramping in her abdomen came with increasing ferocity. Worse, she didn't want to leave Chase. "What about you?"

"I'm going to put a stop to this once and for all." Giving her a final look, he set his hands on her shoulders and pointed her toward the barn. "Run," he whispered, and then turned in the direction from which they'd come.

Chapter Twelve

Chase didn't want to leave Lily unprotected. Damn it, he didn't want her out of his sight. But he knew both of them would stand a better chance if he went on the offensive. He couldn't do that with her in tow. Running was her best chance of surviving, so he let her go—and prayed to God he could stop the men with guns before they got to her.

He sprinted back to the Toyota, yanked open the door and jammed his body behind the wheel. Twisting the key, he pumped the gas. The engine turned over on the first try. Glancing over his shoulder, he spotted the SUV twenty yards away. At some point, it had begun to rain again, but Chase barely noticed. Standing next to the

SUV, two men—one with a rifle, the other with a pistol—started toward him.

Knowing he had only a few seconds before they started blasting, he rammed the shift into gear and floored the accelerator. The tires spun, spewing dirt and gravel high into the air. The car fishtailed. Then the tires grabbed asphalt and shot forward.

The men simultaneously dropped into a shooter's stance. Weapons up, they swung toward the speeding car—and Chase. The first shot blew a hole the size of his fist in the windshield. Cracks in the safety glass spread like spidery veins. Something thwacked against the passenger headrest so close to his head Chase felt the concussion.

But he didn't stop. He knew the odds were high that he would get shot before he mowed them down. But Chase was nearly out of ammo. His most powerful weapon at the moment was the car, and he intended to put it to good use.

The windshield imploded. Glass pelted him. Through the gaping hole, he saw the men scatter. Chase cut the wheel and went after the man with the rifle. A sniper was always the most dangerous.

The rifleman turned and ran toward the ditch on the opposite side of the road, but he was no match for the speeding car. Using every driving skill he'd amassed over the years, Chase took the car into the ditch after the gunman. The man jumped on a three-rail fence and tried to scale it to escape into a cornfield. Under any other circumstances, Chase would have tried to take him alive to glean information from him later. Tonight, all he cared about was keeping Lily safe.

He floored the accelerator and the engine roared as the car bounced over rough ground. Midway over the fence, the gunman turned and raised his hands as if to protect himself. Chase hit the brake, but the vehicle skidded the rest of the way through dirt and grass. It struck both the fence and the gunman. Wood splintered and flew high into the air. The impact sent the man twenty feet into the field. He didn't get up.

One down and one to go, Chase thought as he rammed the car into Reverse. He hadn't noticed that the engine had died.

He turned the key and pumped the gas, but the motor only groaned. Throwing open the door, he hit the ground, running toward the downed man to confiscate the rifle.

He was almost there when a gunshot split the air. The bullet kicked up dirt inches from Chase's right foot. When he didn't stop, a second shot tore through the material of his slacks. Chase skidded to a halt.

"Game over," said a voice from behind him. "Get your hands up, Vickers."

The unmistakable sound of a pistol being cocked froze his blood in his veins. Chase couldn't believe the man had gotten the drop on him. *You're getting sloppy, Vickers.*

Chase raised his hands and slowly turned. Even with his hair wet from the falling rain, he recognized the man. The same man who'd ambushed him in the limo back at Hancock Tower.

"So we meet again," the man said.

"Who the hell are you and what do you want?"

"You, my friend. This is all about you. And the woman, of course." The man smiled, his eyes scanning the surrounding darkness. "She couldn't have gotten far now, could she?" His smile chilled Chase. "I take it the baby is yours?"

Chase wanted to rip him apart with his bare hands, but he shoved the emotions aside. In this business, emotions were what got people killed.

"I have no ties to her or the kid," he lied, desperate to buy time. If his calculations were correct, he had one bullet left in the pistol. If they were going to get out of this alive, he was going to have to make it count.

"Valiant effort, *Vic*. But you see, I've been a good boy. I did my homework. I know all about you and Ms. Garrett."

"Then you know we've been through for a long time."

The other man smiled. "Then you won't mind too much when I put a bullet in her, will you?"

Staving off burgeoning panic, Chase stared at him, his mind scrambling. He couldn't shake the same keen sense of familiarity he'd felt back in Boston. Where had he seen this guy before?

"Do I know you?" Chase asked, stalling.

"Let's just say you know *of* me."

"You're familiar. I'm pretty sure I've seen you before."

"We'd never laid eyes on each other until last night."

"If we've never met, then what's this all about?"

Even in the darkness Chase saw hatred flash in the other man's eyes. "I'm merely repaying a debt."

"For who?" Willing his nerves to settle, Chase sidled closer. "Your father?"

"Don't be a hero. Drop your weapon and kick it toward me."

"Which son are you?"

"Get back."

Chase inched closer. "Tell me why you're doing this. If you're going to kill me, anyway, I deserve to know that much."

The man assumed a shooter's stance. "I'll kill you where you stand, you backstabbing bastard. And then I'll kill the woman. I'll put a bullet right through her belly. Right through the baby. And I'll make sure you're conscious so you can watch her bleed out."

Rage mingled with cold, hard fear and

spread through Chase's body like ice water running through his veins. The first rule of military or law enforcement was that you never gave up your weapon. He didn't intend to break that golden rule, but if it came down to Lily's life or giving up his weapon, what could he do?

"In a few minutes," Chase said, "this place is going to be crawling with cops."

A chilling smile overtook the man's face. "Then I guess I'd better hurry things along and get this show on the road."

With lightning-fast speed, the man shifted the gun and fired. Shock stabbed Chase. White-hot pain knifed through his right hand all the way to his elbow. Instinctively, he used his left hand to grasp his injured right. When he looked down and saw blood, another layer of fear enveloped him.

"What the hell did you do that for?" Chase snarled between clenched teeth.

"That was for my father." The man aimed the gun at his groin. "This one is for you."

"Wait!" Chase shouted. "Tell me why! Tell me who you are!"

"Aidan Shea, bro." He relaxed his grip

on the gun. "I'm the man who's going to send you to hell."

"Why me? I barely knew your father."

"You knew him well enough to frame him. You and your so-called band of brothers sent him to prison for something he didn't do. Do you have any idea what that did to him?"

"I had no part in that."

"Tell it to Satan, you lying bastard." He took aim, the muzzle leveled on Chase's abdomen.

Chase braced, expecting the impact of a bullet and mind-numbing pain. But he couldn't stop thinking about Lily. This man was going to disable him, then he was going to kill her while Chase watched. He'd do anything to stop the horrific scenario. But what?

The only sound on the road was the pounding of his heart. Till the gunshot split the quiet.

His nerves jumped, and instinctively, he stumbled back, raising his hands in a useless effort to protect himself. But there was no need.

Aidan Shea crumpled to the ground.

Chase stared, disbelief and relief barreling through him in equal measure. His knees nearly buckled when he turned to find Lily standing twenty feet away, the rifle in her hands.

"Lily…"

He heard her name, realized belatedly he'd whispered it. Her gaze shifted to his. Worry skittered through him when he saw the distant look in her eyes. Her face was ghastly pale; tears glistened on her cheeks. She took a single step toward him, the rifle clattering to the ground.

Then he was running toward her, enveloping her in his arms. Her body trembled violently against him. He held her tight, wanting to calm her, protect her, thank her for saving his life. Smoothing her hair away from her face with his uninjured hand, he marveled at her beauty. At the softness of her body, so warm and blessedly alive against his.

"Are you okay?" he asked when he found his voice.

"I killed him," she choked out.

"I know, honey." He held her tighter. "I'm sorry you had to do that. He didn't give you any choice."

"He was going to kill you." Her body vibrated against his.

"You did what you had to do." When she only sobbed, he held her tighter. "You're going to be okay. I promise."

Worried that she could be going into shock, he eased her to arm's length and set his hand against her face. "Shh. Easy does it. It's okay." But Chase knew firsthand how difficult it was to use lethal force. Even for soldiers and secret agents, no matter how tough or seemingly emotionally detached, it wounded the soul to take a life.

"You saved my life," he said quietly.

Her focus went to his hand, where blood dripped from his fingertips. "Oh, Chase, you're bleeding."

"I don't think it's too bad." The wound throbbed with every beat of his heart, but Chase was just thankful to be alive. "Let's get you to the car," he said. "I'm going to search the men and see if I can get a phone to call nine-one-one."

She nodded. But he could see her lips quivering. Her teeth beginning to chatter. More than anything, he wanted to get her to a place where she could decompress. A place where he could take care of her.

Alarm shot through him when she gasped and doubled over.

"Lily! What is it?"

"Just...a cramp, I think."

"The baby?"

"I don't know. It's too soon." Another gasp escaped her. "Maybe."

AIDAN SHEA COULDN'T BELIEVE he was going to die this way. Gut shot by a pregnant woman and bleeding out on some godforsaken road in the middle of nowhere. He had so much more to do. How had things gone so terribly wrong? If only he could complete this leg of the mission and eliminate Vickers. Ethan Matalon and Ty Jones had been next, but Aidan knew his brothers and father would take care of them.

With the last of his breath, Aidan cursed Chase Vickers. He cursed Ethan and Ty and all of the others who'd been involved. He'd wanted to finish Vickers himself. But he knew the most important phase of the plan had already been set into motion. The bomb he'd planted. No one knew about it, other than him and his brothers and father, and no one could stop it.

And the clock was ticking….

The knowledge comforted him in a way nothing else could. He smiled through the pain of the gunshot wound, and he tasted blood. It should have been their blood, but it was his own. No matter. Soon they would be dead and his father would be avenged.

Revenge was such a powerful motivator.

Now it was time to get down to the business of dying. Such a slow process. In the near distance Aidan could hear Vickers and the woman, and another wave of fury washed over him. Damn them to hell, he thought. Damn all of them.

A groan escaped him when he shifted. The pain had receded slightly. That was when he realized he still had the gun in his hand. That he could still move.

And he smiled.

"HANG ON." Chase scooped Lily into his arms. She was amazingly lightweight. He reveled in her warmth as he carried her across the road toward the ditch where he'd left the Toyota.

They were midway to the car when a gunshot rent the air. Chase stopped, his heart dropping into his stomach.

"Put her down, Vickers!"

Chase spun to see Aidan Shea standing a few yards away, his pistol leveled on Chase. Blood oozed from his chest, shiny and red, staining his clothes in an expanding circle. Still, Chase set Lily on her feet.

"This ends here and now," Shea said as he shifted the pistol and took aim at Lily.

"No!" Chase threw himself in front of her, but he wasn't fast enough. The blast fractured the air and Lily fell to the ground. "No!" he screamed. *"No!"*

Out of the corner of his eye he saw Aidan Shea's body jerk. He spun around and fired three times in quick succession before crumpling to the ground. At first, Chase thought he'd succumbed to the bullet wound he'd sustained earlier. Then he spotted the other figure just beyond. Before Chase could identify him, the man staggered, then fell to the ground. What the hell? Another gunman? Chase considered trying to get off a shot with his left hand. But he needed to tend to Lily first.

Dropping to his knees beside her, he ran his uninjured hand over her, searching for a bullet wound, for blood. Her eyes were open, watching him. She was crying. Obviously in pain. *Oh, dear God, please let her survive this.*

"Honey," he choked. "Where are you hit?"

"I'm not." She took his hand. "I think it's the baby."

"Vickers!" a familiar voice called out.

Chase fumbled for his pistol with his left hand, surged to his feet and spun

Realization dawned in a rush. Ben Parker had arrived just in time. He'd shot Aidan Shea and saved their lives. Now he was down with a gunshot wound.

"Stay put," Chase said to Lily, then he started toward the fallen man.

"About time you showed up," Chase said when he came upon Ben.

"Timing was off just a little."

Chase knelt beside the FBI agent, noticed the shiny slick of blood on the asphalt. "How bad are you hit?"

"Not looking too good. Bastard got me in the chest."

Chase grabbed Ben's cell phone and quickly dialed nine-one-one, asking for the police and two ambulances.

When he was finished, he looked down at Ben, then took his hand. "How did you find us?"

"There's only one major highway that runs from Boston to Shane's place. Didn't take a rocket scientist to figure it out."

"That's possibly how Shea found us, too." Chase squeezed his friend's hand. How had he ever doubted Ben's loyalty? "You got here just in time."

"Looks that way." Ben's eyes went to Lily. "She okay?"

"I think she's in labor."

Even through the grimace of pain, Ben smiled. "You better get over there."

Chase squeezed his hand again. "You saved our lives, bro."

"Just doing my job."

"Ambulance will be here any moment."

"Go," Ben said.

Chase didn't want to leave him—Ben Parker was in a bad way. But Lily needed him, too.

Taking off his shirt, Chase covered Ben with it to help keep him from going into shock. "I'll be right over there," he said.

"By the way…" Ben closed his eyes. "Congratulations."

Chase gave the man's hand a final squeeze, then strode quickly to where Lily lay on the ground and knelt beside her. "An ambulance is on the way."

"I don't think your daughter is going to wait."

"What?" He'd heard—he just couldn't believe it.

"The baby is coming."

"You mean right now? Here?"

A faint smile touched her lips. "She's impatient, just like her dad."

Alarm and a good measure of fear

rattled through Chase at the thought of helping to deliver his own baby. An EMT, he knew the basic mechanics of labor and delivery, but there were so many things that could go wrong. "I've never done this before," he blurted.

"I did it once in the emergency room," she said. "The baby was very determined and came before the doc could get there. I'll coach—" She bit off the words. Her face screwed up and sweat beaded on her forehead. "It's…going to happen right now."

"Tell me what to do." His voice came out strong, but panic bubbled inside him.

Lily was already in the throes of another contraction. Chase forced his mind back to his EMT training. He knew that when the contractions came at close intervals, delivery time was near.

When the contraction passed, Lily blew out a breath, then began to breathe the way expectant mothers were taught to breathe in Lamaze classes. "I'm taking you to the car," he said, kneeling to scoop her into his arms.

"The backseat. I need to lie down. See if you can find a blanket…"

Chase already had her in his arms. The pain in his injured hand forgotten, he quickly carried her to the car and opened the rear door. "We're in luck," he said, laying her down. "There's a blanket."

"For the baby," she said.

"Okay." Standing at the door, Chase glanced back at the road, wondering where the ambulance was.

"Will you be all right for a moment while I check on Ben?" he asked.

"I'm between contractions." She smiled when he squeezed her hand. "Go."

Chase sprinted toward the downed agent, praying the other man was going to be all right. "Ben?"

The FBI agent raised his head. "What the hell are you doing over here? Get back to that woman, Vickers. She needs you more than I do."

Still, Chase was torn. The man was ghastly pale. His breathing was shallow and rapid. "Hang tight, man. Ambulance should be here any moment."

Ben waved him off, then let his hand

fall back to his side. Praying the other man survived his wounds, Chase sprinted back toward Lily.

PAIN SCREAMED through her with the ferocity of a wild beast raging through her body. Lily braced against the onslaught and pushed with all of her might. Just as the contraction ended, Chase appeared at the car door.

"The baby is coming," she said as she panted.

"What do I do?"

Another contraction tore through her before she could answer. Lily squeezed her eyes shut and rode the wave of agony. At the crest, she used its momentum and pushed until her breath ran out.

When the pain passed, she propped herself up on her elbows and made eye contact with Chase. "Get the blanket ready."

She could feel another contraction approaching and spoke quickly. "When I push next time, the baby's head may appear. Support her head. Don't pull. I'll do the rest."

Pain knifed through her with such power that Lily felt her eyes roll back. A scream hovered in her throat, but she swallowed it. Instead, she used every last bit of her energy to push her baby into the world.

She tried panting, the way she'd learned in her childbirth classes. But nothing could have prepared her for this. A keening sound tore from her lips, till the pain took her breath away.

"I see her!"

Grinding her teeth, Lily accepted the pain, used it to tell her what to do next, and she pushed harder. The contractions came now one on top of the other. No time to rest in between. All she could think about was holding her daughter in her arms for the first time.

"Keep pushing," Chase cooed. "You're doing great, honey. She's coming."

An elongated moan escaped her. The pain rolled lower, wrapping around her lower back and pelvis like a red-hot chain growing ever tighter.

In the next instant, a faint cry sounded. Lily raised her head and looked down to see Chase holding her squirming, supremely unhappy little girl.

She looked at Chase and, for the first time since she'd known him, she saw tears his eyes. He cradled the baby with the reverence of a man holding the most precious thing in the world. In this case, he was.

"She's perfect," he whispered.

A sob broke from Lily's lips. But it was the sound of a mother's joy. As Chase laid the child at her breast, emotion overwhelmed her.

"She's beautiful," she whispered through her tears.

The world shifted on its axis as Lily put her arms around her baby girl and cradled her gently. "Hi there," she whispered. "Welcome to the world, little girl."

"Is she all right?" Chase asked.

"She's got good color and a strong cry." Lily couldn't stop looking at her child. "She seems to be just fine."

Chase wiped his eyes. "She's definitely got a healthy set of lungs."

Lily choked out a laugh. As a nurse, she knew a baby's lungs were the last organs to fully develop. Even though her baby had come early, she appeared to be entirely healthy.

"She's cranky," she said to Chase, then looked back at the child in her arms. "I can't blame you, baby girl."

Chase leaned close, and Lily realized she wasn't the only one who couldn't take her eyes off the baby. Neither could he. "How are you feeling?" he asked.

"Better than I've been in a long time," she said.

He took her hand and squeezed. "We have a daughter."

Lily looked down at the wrinkle-faced little girl. "She looks like you."

Chase made a face and she laughed. "She's got a few more wrinkles."

For a moment the sound of their laughter filled the car.

"Have you thought of a name?" he asked.

"I was thinking of Chassidy."

"Chassidy," he repeated. "I like it."

In the distance, sirens blared. Lily cradled her baby girl, thankful she was safe and alive and healthy. Chase hovered over her, like the new father he was. He hadn't taken his eyes off either of them.

As the first ambulance arrived and the EMTs disembarked, Chase gave her hand a final squeeze and met her eyes. Within their depths, Lily saw all the things she'd always known in her heart. He loved her. She loved him, too. She always would. But she knew it wasn't enough to change who he was or what he did.

The thought of him walking away, of her never seeing him again, was like a giant hand reaching into her and yanking her heart from her chest.

"I'm going to check on Ben," Chase said.

Lily thought she saw something now in his eyes. Something vague, unsettling and slightly sad that she didn't quite understand. It was as if he'd closed himself off emotionally.

"Thank him for me." She looked down at her precious baby. "Thank him for both of us."

Chase nodded and gave her a smile. But as he turned and walked away, all Lily could think was that she was never going to see him again.

Chapter Thirteen

Chase had always prided himself on having the integrity to do the right thing, even when the right thing wasn't necessarily the easy thing. He'd learned at an impressionable age to take the high road over the low. He'd always been a firm believer in the adage that adversity built character.

For the first time in his adult life he was tempted to take the easy way out. To hell with his self-imposed code of honor. But he also knew a relationship with Lily, and with his infant daughter, would be anything but easy. As much as he didn't want to face it, Chase was going to have to walk away from both of them.

He hadn't seen Lily since he'd delivered her baby—*their* baby—a few hours ago. It felt more like years. Better get used to it, a harsh voice reminded him. But it had taken him that long to muster the nerve to do what he needed to do.

He and Lily had made statements to both the police and the FBI. Chase found out later that Aidan Shea had died at the scene. The nightmare should have been over.

But Chase knew Liam Shea and his other sons were still out there. And they would like nothing more than to hurt the people Chase loved most.

The authorities were looking for them, but the Sheas were still at large. A fact that brought Chase's line of thinking full circle.

The truth of the matter was he'd made a lot of enemies in the years he'd been with Eclipse. Too many, if he wanted to be honest about it. He had no way of knowing if—or when—one of them would reappear. All he could do now was protect what he loved most. In this case, the two people who meant the most to Chase: Lily and his daughter. In order to keep them safe, he had to sever ties with them once and for all. He had to end it right here and now.

It was going to kill him to walk away. It had only been a few hours since he'd last seen Lily, since he'd last spoken to her, heard her voice, touched her skin, and already he felt he was dying inside. She was the one great love of his life. He would never love another the way he loved her.

And then there was Chassidy. One look at his precious little girl and Chase had been a goner. She had Lily's red hair and his nose. Already he loved her more than his own life. How was he going to walk away? How could he live his life without them?

The ache went clean through his chest as he walked into the lobby of New Hampshire Medical Center, a small local hospital just twenty miles from Shane's house. He took the elevator to the maternity ward. He promised himself he wasn't going to look in on Chassidy. This would be easier if he didn't let things get too complicated. But as he passed the glassed-in nursery, the sight of a dozen or more screaming, squirming babies stopped him dead in his tracks.

His eyes were drawn immediately to the crib with the pink zebra blanket and the name "Garrett" printed on the placard. He couldn't keep the stupid grin off his face as he ogled the baby inside. *His* little girl.

In the past, babies had always been more like small, mysterious and screaming alien beings. Tonight, he felt a connection to the little girl such as he'd never before experienced in his life.

A man standing a few feet away wearing blue jeans and a T-shirt snagged Chase's attention. Disbelief swept through him when the man turned and he saw his half brother, Shane.

Chase was surprised all over again when his half brother grinned. "Which one is she, bro?"

Chase's heart tripped, his pulse rate jacked at seeing Shane here. "Uh, the little girl on the right. In the zebra blanket."

"Ah, the little redhead. I should have known. Too damn cute to be yours."

"Takes after her mom."

"Good thing, I guess."

"Yeah." Staring at his daughter, pride

swelled in his chest with such power that for a moment Chase couldn't draw a breath.

The baby kicked her little legs and let out a squeal loud enough to make both men jump. Chase couldn't help it; he grinned at the toothless, screaming, red-faced baby girl.

"Takes after you, that's for sure," Shane said.

Chase looked into his brother's eyes. The same eyes he'd looked into as a hurt and angry ten-year-old boy and had seen the man he'd once wanted to be someday. But that man had walked out on him. Left him alone and in the hands of strangers.

Reaching into his pocket, Shane withdrew a cigar and offered it to Chase. "Congratulations, man."

"Thanks." Chase didn't smoke, but he took the cigar.

"How's Lily?"

"Good." He glanced toward the hall and he wondered how things would go between them. "I'm about to see her."

"Tell her I said congratulations."

"I'll do that."

Shane stuck out his hand. His dark eyes burned into Chase's. "I'm happy for you, man."

Chase hesitated for an instant, then grasped his brother's hand and shook it hard. "Thanks."

"I thought maybe I might be a real uncle…and a brother."

"I think maybe you could." Chase knew the old wounds would not heal overnight, but this was a step in the right direction. "See you around."

"Bet on it."

Chase slid the cigar into his pocket and started toward Lily's room.

He found her standing near the window, looking out at the city beyond. Her hair was down, the red tresses curling around her shoulders. If he didn't know better, he never would have believed she'd had a baby just hours ago.

She turned then, and the sight of her face struck him like a punch to his solar plexus, literally taking his breath away. Her green eyes widened when she noticed him standing in the doorway of her room. Her lips parted, but it was as if his presence had rendered her speechless.

"Chase," she whispered.

He entered the room and stopped. "Hi."

"Hi."

"How are you feeling?"

"Really good."

"How's Chassidy?"

"The doctor says she's just fine." She fumbled with the collar of her robe. "Any word on the blackout?"

"The city is still without power," he said. "The damage at the power stations was pretty extensive. It's probably going to be a while."

She looked strong and capable as she stood there, contemplating him. But he'd seen her at her most vulnerable. The image of her bringing their baby into the world flashed in his mind's eye. It was the most profound moment of his life. One he would never forget for as long as he lived.

"You look good," he said.

"So do you." She sent a pointed look to his bandaged hand. "How is it?"

"No permanent damage."

"I'm glad." She fiddled with her collar again.

"I stopped in the nursery and looked in on Chassidy," he said.

Her full lips curved into a smile that made his heart stumble in his chest. "She's beautiful, isn't she?"

"Just like her mom."

"Her dad's not too bad to look at, either."

Chase laughed outright at that. He was a lot of things, but he'd never even conceived of the idea of beautiful.

"How's Ben?" she asked.

A shadow of grief passed over Chase's heart. While his daughter had come into the world, Ben Parker had passed away from the gunshot wound. Grimacing, he shook his head. "He didn't make it."

Lily's hand went to her mouth. Her eyes filled, but she didn't cry. "I'm sorry."

"He died a hero. That's the way he would have wanted it."

"That's so unfair. He saved our lives." She blinked back tears, a breath shuddering out of her. "So did you."

This was the moment he should bring up the harsh fact that he had also been the one to bring danger into their lives. For the life of him, Chase couldn't do it. He loved Lily. He loved Little Chassidy. He wanted to be part of their lives. God knows it was going to kill him to walk away.

As if realizing there were too many things that had been left unsaid between them, Lily turned back to the window. "I didn't know if you'd come."

"I tried to stay away." Taking a deep breath, he crossed to her. "I couldn't do it."

Even from two feet away he could smell the soft scent of her. Something warm and floral and sweet that titillated his senses. He wanted badly to reach out and touch her. He wanted even more to pull her into his arms and never let her go.

Finally, she turned to face him. For an interminable moment, they stared into each other's eyes, a hundred thoughts zinging between them.

"I came to say goodbye," Chase managed after a moment.

An emotion he couldn't identify flashed

in Lily's eyes. Relief? Pain? Willingness to face the hard facts even when he wasn't?

"Chase…"

"I'd like to support Chassidy financially, if it's all right with you." Before he lost his nerve, he cut off the protest he saw in her eyes and continued. "It's important to me, Lily. I can set up a trust for her. For college, maybe. Med school. Law school. Whatever she wants. I'll make everything anonymous so it can never be traced back to me."

Instead of arguing, Lily simply nodded. "All right."

"I wish I could do more," he said. *Like watch my daughter grow up and share it with the woman I love.* "I want to take responsibility for my part."

"I agree," she said.

He wanted to say more, but the words jammed in his throat. He knew anything he said now would probably do nothing but get him in deeper than he already was. But, dear God, he didn't want to leave. He couldn't imagine turning and walking out that door, never to see either of them again.

He stood there, drinking in the image of

the woman he loved more than his own life. He branded the picture of her onto his brain—soft red hair, cautious green eyes, skin as soft as velvet—and reminded himself he would always have his memories of her. They were going to have to be enough.

They would never be enough.

"I've got to go," he heard himself say. "Before I do something we're both going to regret."

Taking a final, lingering look at Lily, he turned and started toward the door.

"DON'T GO."

Lily hadn't meant to say the words aloud. Her heart had been chanting them like a mantra and somehow they had bubbled to the surface.

Chase stopped before reaching the door, but he didn't turn to her. Though she couldn't see his face, Lily saw clearly the war raging within him. The battle between duty and love, right and wrong. Chase lived in a world of black and white. She knew reality's boundaries were rarely that clear. She couldn't help but wonder if there was some middle ground they might be able to find.

After a moment, he drew a breath and turned to her. His eyes were shuttered and hard. His mouth pulled into a frown. "I have to go," he said.

"I'm not finished."

He went rigid when she started toward him. Lily watched him steel himself against her closeness. Against all the things they'd shared. She knew he loved her. She knew he would always love her. But was love enough?

It devastated her knowing he was willing to walk away to keep her safe. To keep Chassidy safe. That was the kind of man Chase Vickers was. The kind of man who would sacrifice his needs to do the right thing. He was the kind of man she had fallen in love with.

How could he expect her to let him go? Was his work so important that he was willing to sacrifice what they had?

"I don't think it's going to help our

situation if we draw this thing out," he said.

She stopped a foot away from him and shook her head. "I never had you pegged as a coward, Vickers, but then this isn't the first time in the course of our relationship that you've surprised me."

He blinked. "Excuse me?"

"And it's not the first time you've run." She squared her shoulders. "You're willing to take on some of the most vicious killers in the world, and yet when it comes to your own daughter and the woman you claim to love, you turn tail and run."

He looked truly offended. "It's the only way to keep you safe," he said. "Look at what we've been through."

"We've been through a terrible ordeal I would never want to repeat," she shot back. "But guess what? There are no guarantees in this life, Chase. Do you think a love like what we share happens more than once?" Raising her hand, she poked him in the chest with her index finger hard enough to send him back a step. "Let me answer that for you with an unequivocal no. There are no guarantees. No safety nets. No insurance policies for tragedy. I know—I've seen all of those things in the emergency room. Complete strangers whose misfortunes touch me deeply. Just last week a man with a wife and two kids wrecked his car on his way to play golf. His family never saw him alive again."

She poked him again and Chase went back another step. "Do you think he was unlucky? No. You want to know who the unlucky people are, Chase? They're the ones who never find the one great love of their lives."

Some of her anger leached away and she dropped her hand. "We're the lucky ones, Chase. We found something special and precious and rare. Now you want to walk away because you think something bad might happen to me or Chassidy?"

"If it's in my power to keep you safe, then I'm going to do it."

"At what cost?"

Stepping close to her, Chase gently grasped both her biceps and spoke urgently. "This has nothing to do with personal sacrifice or right or wrong. It has to do with making sure that no one hurts our daughter, and that her mother is alive to raise her."

"I have a say in the matter."

"No, you don't."

"What about her father, Chase? Doesn't he count?"

Blinking, he searched her face. "I don't like this any more than you do. But I'm willing to sacrifice what we have to ensure both of you long and safe lives."

"Or maybe you're willing to run away because it's easier than handing over your heart to us. Maybe it's easier to walk away from us than it would be for you to walk away from your work."

Her own words shocked her to silence.

"There's nothing even remotely easy about any of this," he ground out.

"Then do the right thing. Listen to your heart. Listen to mine. Give your daughter a father."

Unable to keep himself from it, Chase pulled her into his arms and held her so tightly he thought he must be bruising her. He could feel his emotions winding up, like a giant rubber band tightening in his chest and squeezing his heart and lungs until he couldn't breathe.

"That scares the hell out of me," he said.

"Life isn't about safe."

He smiled. "There's some irony in there somewhere."

She smiled back. "Lots of it."

He scrubbed a hand over his jaw. "There are no guarantees someone won't emerge from my past. I've made some serious enemies over the years."

"Get out while you can. Let the other men cover your back. You've given them years of your life. I want the rest of it, and I'm not willing to share."

The dark cloud that had been hovering lifted. Could he rely on his Eclipse brothers to keep the Sheas at bay? The answer, he realized, was an unequivocal yes.

Chase stared at Lily, loving her so much he could barely draw a breath. "You're pretty damn smart for a civilian."

"I like to think so."

When she looked at him like that, with

a sultry smile and hooded eyes, he never could resist her. He couldn't now.

Chase grinned. "Honey, I think I've run my last mission."

"Are you sure?"

"More sure of that than anything else in my life."

Lily's smile widened and she let out a contented sigh. The sound was like music to Chase's ears. The sound of simple human joy, as fleeting and precious as a sunrise.

"This will be a fresh start for us," she said.

"A new start as a family." Setting his hands on either side of her face, he kissed her mouth, her cheeks, the tip of her nose. "I love you."

"I love you, too," she whispered. "I never stopped."

Lily glanced at the door, where two nurses stared at them, teary eyed, and she laughed at the picture she and Chase must make. "I think it's time to go get our daughter," she said.

"I think you're right," Chase replied.

The nurses both winked at Lily as she

and Chase walked hand in hand to the door. Lily winked back as they strode toward their precious daughter and the promise of a new life together as a family.

* * * * *

*Turn the page for a sneak peek
at the thrilling continuation
of the* LIGHTS OUT *continuity.*
ANYTHING FOR HIS SON
by Rita Herron.
On sale in August.
LIGHTS OUT: *Mystery and passion
thrive in the dark…*

Chapter One

Finn Shea smiled as the afternoon temperature in the darkened city began to climb. People were frantic. Traffic jams clogged the streets. Subways had been stranded. A half-million people were without power. Businesses had closed or were trying to run on auxiliary sources. Tempers had flared and violence had broken out, escalating crime.

His father, Liam, had set his plan in motion full swing. The target—the men who belonged to a secretive group called Eclipse, and had been formed   a select coterie of Special Forces servicemen. The name had been chosen by Shane Peters, their security expert, based on the fact that the quartet could "eclipse" anyone, anytime. Only a handful of top-level Pentagon advisers had known about them, and even then, no one had known the identity of the men on the team.

The band of brothers, mercenaries for the good, still performed high-profile, very classified government-sanctioned missions.

Eleven years ago their mission had been to rescue hostages in a civil-war-torn Middle Eastern nation.

A mission that had ended his father's brilliant career.

And ruined his life.

Now his father was out of jail and back in control. Ready to mete out punishments for the men who had betrayed him and stood idly by while he alone took the fall for the disastrous mission.

Commander Tom Bradley had been in charge, but he was dead now. The other six men had moved on, had lived good lives while his father had suffered.

Shane Peters, security expert. Chase

Vickers, engine expert. Ethan Matalon, computer ace. Ty Jones, demolitions man. The only non-American, Frederick LeBron, a language specialist and a king from the tiny Alpine nation of Beau Pays. And last but not least, Grant Davis, then the tactical expert—now the damn vice president.

Actions had already been taken against Shane Peters and Chase Vickers. Vice President Grant Davis…he had no idea what his fate held. And Ethan Matalon was next on the hit list. Finn's target.

Yes, Finn's father, Liam, was finally exacting his revenge.

Because Liam Shea had been innocent. But he'd been court-martialed, dishonorably discharged and incarcerated anyway. And his family's life had been destroyed. His mother had filed for divorce. Hoping to escape the publicity and shame, she'd dragged her sons to that god-awful small town in Oregon.

But they hadn't escaped at all. Finn's father had been tormented every day in prison. And Finn and his brothers…they'd paid the price as well.

Liam's team was to blame.

And now each of them had to face the consequences.

Finn stared at the photo of Ethan Matalon's son, Jesse. Five years old. Without a full-time father. Scared of the dark.

Finn forced a steel wall around his heart. He couldn't care about the kid. Wars caused casualties. An eye for an eye.

And Ethan's Achilles' heel was his son.

It was only fair. Finn's father had lost years with his boys. Ethan would lose his own now, too.

And his pain would be their revenge.

* * * * *

**Every Life Has More
Than One Chapter**

Award-winning author Stevi Mittman
delivers another hysterical mystery,
featuring Teddi Bayer, an irre-
pressible heroine, and her to-die-for
hero, Detective Drew Scoones. After
all, life on Long Island can be murder!

*Turn the page for a sneak peek
at the warm and funny fourth book,
WHOSE NUMBER IS UP, ANYWAY?,
in the Teddi Bayer series,
by STEVI MITTMAN.
On sale August 7*

"Before redecorating a room, I always advise my clients to empty it of everything but one chair. Then I suggest they move that chair from place to place, sitting in it, until the placement feels right. Trust your instincts when deciding on furniture placement. Your room should 'feel right.'"

—TipsFromTeddi.com

Gut feelings. You know, that gnawing in the pit of your stomach that warns you that you are about to do the absolute stupidest thing you could do? Something that will ruin life as you know it?

I've got one now, standing at the butcher counter in King Kullen, the grocery store in the same strip mall as L.I. Lanes, the bowling alley cum billiard parlor I'm in the process of redecorating for its "Grand Opening."

I realize being in the wrong supermarket probably doesn't sound exactly dire to you, but you aren't the one buying your father a brisket at a store your mother will somehow know isn't Waldbaum's.

And then, June Bayer isn't your mother.

The woman behind the counter has agreed to go into the freezer to find a brisket for me, since there aren't any in the case. There are packages of pork tenderloin, piles of spare ribs and rolls of sausage, but no briskets.

Warning Number Two, right? I should be so out of here.

But no, I'm still in the same spot when she comes back out, brisketless, her face ashen. She opens her mouth as if she is going to scream, but only a gurgle comes out.

And then she pinballs out from behind the counter, knocking bottles of Peter Luger Steak Sauce to the floor on her way, now hitting the tower of cans at the end of the prepared foods aisle and sending them sprawling, now making her way down the aisle, careening from side to side as she goes.

Finally, from a distance, I hear her shout, "He's deeeeeaaaad! Joey's deeeeeaaaad."

My first thought is *You should always trust your gut*.

My second thought is that now, somehow, my mother will know I was in King Kullen. For weeks I will have to hear "What did you expect?" as though whenever you go to King Kullen someone turns up dead. And if the detective investigating the case turns out to be Detective Drew Scoones... well, I'll never hear the end of that from her, either.

She still suspects I murdered the guy who was found dead on my doorstep last Halloween just to get Drew back into my life.

Several people head for the butcher's freezer and I position myself to block them. If there's one thing I've learned from finding people dead—and the guy on my doorstep wasn't the first one—it's that the police get very testy when you mess with their murder scenes.

"You can't go in there until the police get here," I say, stationing myself at the end of the butcher's counter and in front of the Employees Only door, acting as if I'm some sort of authority. "You'll contaminate the evidence if it turns out to be murder."

Shouts and chaos. You'd think I'd know better than to throw the word *murder* around. Cell phones are flipping open and tongues are wagging.

I amend my statement quickly. "Which, of course, it probably isn't. Murder, I mean. People die all the time, and it's not always in hospitals or their own beds, or…" I babble when I'm nervous, and the idea of someone dead on the other side of the freezer door makes me very nervous.

So does the idea of seeing Drew Scoones again. Drew and I have this on-again, off-again sort of thing…that I kind of turned off.

Who knew he'd take it so personally when he tried to get serious and I responded by saying we could talk about *us* tomorrow—and then caught a plane to my parents' condo in Boca the next day? In July. In the middle of a job.

For some crazy reason, he took that to mean that I was avoiding him and the subject of *us*.

That was three months ago. I haven't seen him since.

The manager, who identifies himself and points to his nameplate in case I don't believe him, says he has to go into *his cooler*. "Maybe Joey's not dead," he says. "Maybe he can be saved, and you're letting him die in there. Did you ever think of that?"

In fact, I hadn't. But I had thought that the murderer might try to go back in to make sure his tracks were covered, so I say that I will go in and check.

Which means that the manager and I couple up and go in together while everyone pushes against the doorway to peer in, erasing any chance of finding clean prints on that Employees Only door.

I expect to find carcasses of dead animals hanging from hooks, and maybe Joey hanging from one, too. I think it's going to be very creepy and I steel myself, only to find a rather benign series of shelves with large slabs of meat laid out carefully on them, along with boxes and boxes marked simply Chicken.

Nothing scary here, unless you count the body of a middle-aged man with graying hair sprawled faceup on the floor. His eyes are wide open and unblinking. His shirt is stiff. His pants are stiff. His body is stiff. And his expression, you should forgive the pun—is frozen. Bill-the-manager crosses himself and stands mute while I pronounce the guy dead in a sort of *happy now?* tone.

"We should not be in here," I say, and he nods his head emphatically and helps me push people out of the doorway just in time to hear the police sirens and see the cop cars pull up outside the big store windows.

Bobbie Lyons, my partner in Teddi Bayer Interior Designs (and also my neighbor, my best friend and my private fashion police), and Mark, our carpenter (and my dogsitter, confidant and ego booster), rush in from next door. They beat the cops by a half step and shout out my name. People point in my direction.

After all the publicity that followed the unfortunate incident during which I shot my ex-husband, Rio Gallo, and then the subsequent murder of my first client—which I solved, I might add—it seems like the whole world, or at least all of Long Island, knows who I am.

Mark asks if I'm all right. (Did I remember to mention that the man is drop-dead-gorgeous-but-a-decade-too-young-for-me-yet-too-old-for-my-daughter-thank-god?) I don't get a chance to answer him because the police are quickly closing in on the store manager and me.

"The woman—" I begin telling the police. Then I have to pause for the manager to fill in her name, which he does: *Fran*.

I continue. "Right. Fran. Fran went into the freezer to get a brisket. A moment later she came out and screamed that Joey was dead. So I'd say she was the one who discovered the body."

"And you are…?" the cop asks me. It comes out a bit like who do I *think* I am, rather than who am I really?

"An innocent bystander," Bobbie, hair perfect, makeup just right, says, carefully placing her body between the cop and me.

"And she was just leaving," Mark adds. They each take one of my arms.

Fran comes into the inner circle surrounding the cops. In case it isn't obvious from the hairnet and bloodstained white apron with Fran embroidered on it, I explain that she was the butcher who was going for the brisket. Mark and Bobbie take that as a signal that I've done my job and they can now get me out of there. They twist around, with me in the middle, as if we're a Rockettes line, until we are facing away from the butcher counter. They've managed to propel me a few steps toward the exit when disaster—in the form of a Mazda RX7 pulling up at the loading curb—strikes.

Mark's grip on my arm tightens like a vise. "Too late," he says.

Bobbie's expletive is unprintable. "Maybe there's a back door," she suggests, but Mark is right. It's too late.

I've laid my eyes on Detective Scoones. And while my gut is trying to warn me that my heart shouldn't go there, regions farther south are melting at just the sight of him.

"Walk," Bobbie orders me.

And I try to. Really.

Walk, I tell my feet. *Just put one foot in front of the other.*

I can do this because I know, in my heart of hearts, that if Drew Scoones was still interested in me, he'd have gotten in touch with me after I returned from Boca. And he didn't.

Since he's a detective, Drew doesn't have to wear one of those dark blue Nassau County Police uniforms. Instead, he's got on jeans, a tight-fitting T-shirt and a tweedy sports jacket. If you think that sounds good, you should see him. Chiseled features, cleft chin, brown hair that's naturally a little sandy in the front, a smile that…well, that doesn't matter. He isn't smiling now.

He walks up to me, tucks his sunglasses into his breast pocket and looks me over from head to toe.

"Well, if it isn't Miss Cut and Run," he says. "Aren't you supposed to be somewhere in Florida or something?" He looks at Mark accusingly, as if he was covering for me when he told Drew I was gone.

"Detective Scoones?" one of the uniforms says. "The stiff's in the cooler and the woman who found him is over there." He jerks his head in Fran's direction.

Drew continues to stare at me.

You know how when you were young, your mother always told you to wear clean underwear in case you were in an accident? And how, a little farther on, she told you not to go out in hair rollers because you never knew who you might see—or who might see you? And how now your best friend says she wouldn't be caught dead without makeup and suggests you shouldn't either?

Okay, today, *finally*, in my overalls and Converse sneakers, I get it.

I brush my hair out of my eyes. "Well, I'm back," I say. As if he hasn't known my exact whereabouts. The man is a detective, for heaven's sake. "Been back awhile."

Bobbie has watched the exchange and apparently decided she's given Drew all the time he deserves. "And we've got work to do, so…" she says, grabbing my arm and giving Drew a little two-fingered wave goodbye.

As I back up a foot or two, the store manager sees his chance and places himself in front of Drew, trying to get his attention. Maybe what makes Drew such a good detective is his ability to focus.

Only what he's focusing on is me.

"Phone broken? Carrier pigeon died?" he asks me, taking in Fran, the manager, the meat counter and that Employees Only door, all without taking his eyes off me.

Mark tries to break the spell. "We've got work to do there, you've got work to do here, Scoones," Mark says to him, gesturing toward next door. "So it's back to the alley for us."

Drew's lip twitches. "You working the alley now?" he says.

"If you'd like to follow me," Bill-the-manager, clearly exasperated, says to Drew—who doesn't respond. It's as if waiting for my answer is all he has to do.

So, fine. "You knew I was back," I say.

The man has known my whereabouts every hour of the day for as long as I've known him. And my mother's not the only one who won't buy that he "just happened" to answer this particular call. In fact, I'm willing to bet my children's lunch money that he's taken every call within ten miles of my home since the day I got back.

And now he's gotten lucky.

"*You* could have called *me*," I say.

"You're the one who said *tomorrow* for our talk and then flew the coop, chickie," he says. "I figured the ball was in your court."

"Detective?" the uniform says. "There's something you ought to see in here."

Drew gives me a look that amounts to *in or out?*

He could be talking about the investigation, or about our relationship.

Bobbie tries to steer me away. Mark's fists are balled. Drew waits me out, knowing I won't be able to resist what might be a murder investigation.

Finally he turns and heads for the cooler.

And, like a puppy dog, I follow.

Bobbie grabs the back of my shirt and pulls me to a halt.

"I'm just going to show him something," I say, yanking away.

"Yeah," Bobbie says, pointedly looking at the buttons on my blouse. The two at breast level have popped. "That's what I'm afraid of."

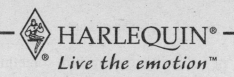

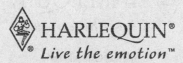

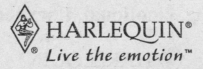

Harlequin® Historical
Historical Romantic Adventure!

*Imagine a time of chivalrous
knights and unconventional ladies,
roguish rakes and impetuous
heiresses, rugged cowboys
and spirited frontierswomen—
these rich and vivid tales will
capture your imagination!*

*Harlequin Historical . . .
they're too good to miss!*